PENGUIN CLASSICS
Maigret Sets a Trap

'I love reading Simenon. He m[...]
– William Faulkner

'A truly wonderful writer . . . marvellously readable – lucid, simple, absolutely in tune with the world he creates'
– Muriel Spark

'Few writers have ever conveyed with such a sure touch, the bleakness of human life'
– A. N. Wilson

'One of the greatest writers of the twentieth century . . . Simenon was unequalled at making us look inside, though the ability was masked by his brilliance at absorbing us obsessively in his stories'
– *Guardian*

'A novelist who entered his fictional world as if he were part of it'
– Peter Ackroyd

'The greatest of all, the most genuine novelist we have had in literature'
– André Gide

'Superb . . . The most addictive of writers . . . A unique teller of tales'
– *Observer*

'The mysteries of the human personality are revealed in all their disconcerting complexity'
– Anita Brookner

'A writer who, more than any other crime novelist, combined a high literary reputation with popular appeal' – P. D. James

'A supreme writer . . . Unforgettable vividness' – *Independent*

'Compelling, remorseless, brilliant'
– John Gray

'Extraordinary masterpieces of the twentieth century'
– John Banville

Georges Simenon was born on 12 February 1903 in Liège, Belgium, and died in 1989 in Lausanne, Switzerland, where he had lived for the latter part of his life. Between 1931 and 1972 he published seventy-five novels and twenty-eight short stories featuring Inspector Maigret.

Simenon always resisted identifying himself with his famous literary character, but acknowledged that they shared an important characteristic:

> My motto, to the extent that I have one, has been noted often enough, and I've always conformed to it. It's the one I've given to old Maigret, who resembles me in certain points . . . 'understand and judge not'.

Penguin is publishing the entire series of Maigret novels.

GEORGES SIMENON

Maigret Sets a Trap

Translated by SIÂN REYNOLDS

PENGUIN BOOKS

PENGUIN CLASSICS

UK | USA | Canada | Ireland | Australia
India | New Zealand | South Africa

Penguin Books is part of the Penguin Random House group of companies
whose addresses can be found at global.penguinrandomhouse.com.

First published in French as *Maigret tend un piège* by Presses de la Cité 1955
This translation first published 2016
003

Set in Dante MT Std 12.5/15 pt
Typeset by Palimpsest Book Production Limited, Falkirk, Stirlingshire
Printed in Great Britain by Clays Ltd, St Ives plc

ISBN: 978-0-241-24030-4

www.greenpenguin.co.uk

MIX
Paper from
responsible sources
FSC® C018179

Penguin Random House is committed to a
sustainable future for our business, our readers
and our planet. This book is made from Forest
Stewardship Council® certified paper.

Contents

1. Commotion at Quai des Orfèvres

From half past three on, Maigret began to look up now and then at the clock. At ten to four, he initialled the last sheet he had been annotating, pushed back his chair, mopped his brow, and hesitated over his choice from the five pipes in the ashtray which he had smoked without bothering to tap them out afterwards. His foot had pressed the bell under the desk and there was a knock at the door. Patting his face with his voluminous handkerchief, he called out gruffly:

'Come in!'

It was Inspector Janvier who, like him, had taken off his jacket but had kept on his tie, whereas Maigret had removed his.

'Give this to the typist. Have someone bring it for me to sign when it's ready. It has to go to Coméliau this evening.'

It was the 4th of August. The windows were wide open but brought no relief, since they allowed in even more warm air, which seemed to be rising from the melting tarmac, the burning hot stonework, and even the Seine itself: one could imagine the river steaming like a pan of water on a stove.

The taxis and buses on Pont Saint-Michel were moving more slowly than usual, seeming to drag themselves along, and it was not only in the Police Judiciaire that people were in shirt-sleeves: men walking past on the streets were carrying their jackets over their arms, and

Maigret had even noticed one or two wearing shorts, as if they were at the seaside.

Only about a quarter of Parisians had stayed in the capital, and all of them must be thinking with identical longing of the others, the lucky ones who were at this very moment paddling at the edge of the waves, or fishing in the shade on some quiet riverbank.

'Have they got over there yet?'

'Haven't seen them. Lapointe's watching out for them.'

Maigret, as if it took some effort, chose one of the pipes and tapped it out, then conscientiously started packing it, before finally moving over to the window, where he stayed standing, his eyes fixed on a certain café-restaurant on the opposite embankment, Quai des Grands-Augustins. The café façade was painted yellow. Two steps led down into it from the street: the interior would be almost as cool as a cellar. The bar still had a genuine zinc counter of the old-fashioned kind, a slate on the wall with the menu chalked up on it, and inside there was a perpetual smell of calvados.

Even some of the booksellers' stalls along the embankments were padlocked for the holidays!

He remained without moving for four or five minutes, drawing on his pipe, then saw a taxi pull up not far from the little restaurant: three men got out and headed for the steps. The most familiar of the silhouettes was that of Inspector Lognon, from the 18th arrondissement, who, from a distance, seemed even smaller and thinner than usual, and who was, for the first time in Maigret's experience, wearing a panama hat.

What would the three men be drinking? Beer, no doubt.

Maigret pushed open the door of the inspectors' office, where the same torpid atmosphere reigned as in the rest of the city.

'Is the Baron out in the corridor?'

'Has been for half an hour, boss.'

'No other journalists?'

'Young Rougin's just arrived.'

'Any photographers?'

'Just the one.'

The long corridor of the Police Judiciaire was almost empty, with a mere two or three clients waiting outside the doors of Maigret's colleagues. It was at his request that Bodard from the Fraud Squad had summoned for four o'clock the man all the newspapers were talking about, a certain Max Bernat, unknown two weeks ago, and suddenly the central figure in the latest financial scandal, one relating to billions of francs.

Maigret had no business with Bernat. Bodard had no reason to call him in either, at the present stage of the investigation. But because Bodard had casually mentioned that he would be interviewing this known criminal figure at four p.m. that day, at least two reporters who specialized in crime would be there with a photographer. They would stay until the interrogation was over. Perhaps, if word got around that Max Bernat was at Quai des Orfèvres, a few more journalists would turn up.

From the inspectors' office, a slight commotion could be heard at exactly four o'clock, heralding the arrival of the fraudster, who had been brought there from the Santé prison.

Maigret waited another ten minutes, pacing up and

down, smoking his pipe, mopping his face from time to time, and glancing across at the little restaurant on the far side of the Seine, then finally he snapped his fingers and said to Janvier:

'Go ahead!'

Janvier picked up the telephone and dialled the restaurant number. Over there, Lognon must have been waiting next to the cabin, ready to tell the café proprietor:

'It'll be for me. I'm expecting a call.'

Everything was going according to plan. Maigret, treading heavily, and a little anxiously, went back into his own office where, before sitting down, he drew himself a glass of water from the tap over the enamel basin.

Ten minutes later, a familiar scene was unfolding in the corridor. Lognon and another inspector from the 18th, a Corsican by the name of Alfonsi, were slowly climbing the stairs, with a man between them who appeared ill at ease, and was concealing his face with his hat.

The Baron and his colleague Jean Rougin, waiting outside Chief Inspector Bodard's door, needed no more than a glance to take in the scene. They rushed across, as the photographer was already levelling his camera.

'Who's that?'

They knew Lognon. They knew the names of the Paris police almost as well as the staff of their own newspapers. If two inspectors who did not belong to the Police Judiciaire but were stationed in Montmartre were bringing in to Quai des Orfèvres some individual who was hiding his face before he had even seen any journalists, that could only mean one thing.

'Is he for Maigret?'

Lognon did not reply, but headed straight for Maigret's office and knocked discreetly at the door. It opened. The three figures vanished inside. The door closed.

The Baron and Jean Rougin looked at each other with the expressions of men who had just discovered a state secret, knowing that they were both thinking the same thing, but felt no need to comment.

'Get a good snap?' Rougin asked the photographer.

'Except that the hat was hiding his face.'

'All the same. Send it off fast to the paper, and get back here. We don't know when they're likely to come back out.'

Alfonsi emerged almost at once.

'Who was that?' they asked.

The inspector looked awkward.

'I can't tell you anything.'

'Why not?'

'Orders.'

'Where's he from, where did you pick him up?'

'Ask Detective Chief Inspector Maigret.'

'A witness?'

'Don't know.'

'A new suspect?'

'I promise you, I don't know.'

'Thanks a lot for your help!'

'I suppose if it *was* the killer, you'd have handcuffed him?'

Alfonsi walked away with a regretful expression, like a man who would like to say more, the corridor returned to its calm, and for half an hour there were no further comings or goings.

The crook, Max Bernat, came out of the Fraud Squad office, but he had already been relegated by the journalists to secondary importance. They nevertheless put questions to Bodard, as a matter of duty.

'Has he given any names?'

'Not yet.'

'He's denying that certain politicians are involved?'

'He didn't deny anything, and didn't admit anything. He's giving nothing away for now.'

'When will you be questioning him again?'

'When certain facts have been checked.'

Maigret emerged from his office, still without jacket or tie, and headed for the commissioner's office, looking pre-occupied.

This was another sign: despite the holiday season, and despite the heat, the Police Judiciaire was about to experi-ence one of its critical evenings, and the two reporters were thinking about certain interrogations that had lasted all night, in some cases over twenty-four hours, without anyone being able to discover what was going on behind the closed doors.

The photographer was back.

'You didn't tell them anything at the paper, did you?'

'Just told them to develop the film and to keep the prints ready.'

Maigret spent half an hour in the chief's office and returned to his own room, brushing the reporters aside with a weary gesture.

'Can you at least tell us if this is to do with—?'

'I've got nothing to say for the moment.'

At six o'clock, the waiter from the Brasserie Dauphine brought over a tray laden with beers. They had seen Lucas leave his office and go into Maigret's, but he had not re-emerged. They had seen Janvier hurry out, hat on head, and get into one of the police cars down below.

A more unusual development was that Lognon appeared once more and, as Maigret had done, headed for the chief's office. True, he stayed there only ten minutes, after which, instead of leaving, he entered the inspectors' office.

'Did you notice anything?' the Baron asked his colleague.

'The hat he had on when he got here?'

It was hard for them to think of 'Inspector Hard-done-by', as everyone in the police and press corps called him, wearing an almost jaunty straw hat.

'Better than that.'

'He didn't smile though, did he?'

'No. But he's wearing a red tie.'

Lognon invariably wore dark-coloured neckties, fixed on to a celluloid clip.

'So what does that mean?'

The Baron knew everything, and communicated other people's secrets with a thin smile.

'His wife's away on holiday.'

'I thought she was an invalid.'

'She was.'

'Cured, then?'

For years, poor Lognon had been obliged, when not on duty, to do the shopping and cooking, and to clean his apartment on Place Constantin-Pecqueur, as well as taking care of his wife, who had declared herself to be a permanent invalid.

'She's met a new tenant in their building. And this woman told her about the spa at Pougues-les-Eaux, and persuaded her to try taking the waters. Strange as it may seem, she's gone off there, not with her husband, who can't leave Paris right now, but with this neighbour. They're the same age, and the neighbour's a widow . . .'

The shuttling to and fro between offices was becoming more and more frequent. Almost all the men belonging to Maigret's squad had dispersed in different directions. Janvier had returned. Lucas was bustling about, sweat dripping from his brow. Lapointe appeared from time to time, as did Torrence, the newcomer Mauvoisin, and several other officers, whom the reporters tried to buttonhole, but it was impossible to get a word out of any of them.

Young Maguy, a reporter on a morning daily paper, soon arrived: she was looking as fresh as if the temperature had not been 36 degrees in the shade all day.

'What are you doing here?'

'Same as you.'

'And that is?'

'Waiting.'

'How did you know anything was happening?'

She shrugged her shoulders and applied some lipstick.

'How many of them are in there?' she asked, pointing at Maigret's door.

'Five or six. Hard to count them. They keep coming and going. They seem to be taking turns.'

'Putting the screws on him, are they?'

'Well, the man in there must be getting pretty hot under the collar.'

'Did they have beer sent up?'

'Yes.'

That was significant. When Maigret sent for a trayful of beers, it indicated that he thought they would be there for some time.

'Lognon still with them?'

'Yes.'

'Does he look pleased?'

'Hard to tell with him. He's wearing a red tie.'

'Why?'

'His wife's gone off to some spa.'

They understood each other. They belonged to the same confraternity.

'Did you see him?'

'Who?'

'The one they're putting through it.'

'Yes, but not his face. He was hiding behind his hat.'

'Young?'

'Not young, not old. Over thirty at a guess.'

'Dressed how?'

'Like anyone else. What colour was his suit, Rougin?'

'Grey.'

'I'd have said beige.'

'What's he look like?'

'Ordinary, man in the street.'

Steps were heard on the stairs and Maguy murmured as the others looked round:

'Must be my photographer.'

By half past seven, there were five of them from the press in the corridor, and they saw the waiter from the Brasserie Dauphine come up with more beer and some sandwiches.

This time it must be really serious. One after another, the reporters went to a small office at the end of the corridor to telephone to their paper.

'Shall we go and eat?'

'What if he comes out while we're away?'

'What if they're going to be here all night?'

'Shall we send out for some sandwiches too?'

'Good idea!'

'And beer?'

The sun was vanishing behind the rooftops, but it was still light, and if the air wasn't exactly sizzling now, the heat remained just as sultry.

At half past eight, Maigret opened his door, looking exhausted, a lock of hair plastered across his brow. He glanced into the corridor, made as if to walk over to the reporters, but changed his mind and the door closed once more behind him.

'Looks like things are hotting up.'

'I told you we'd be here all night. Were you here when they questioned Mestorino?'

'I was still in short pants.'

'It lasted twenty-seven hours!'

'In August?'

'I don't know what month it was, but . . .'

Maguy's flowered cotton dress was clinging to her figure, dark patches had appeared under her arms and through the fabric the outline of her bra and panties was visible.

'Shall we have a game of belote?'

The lights went on above their heads. Darkness was falling.

The night shift clerk took up his place at the end of the corridor.

'Can we get some air in here?'

He went to open first one of the office doors, then the window, then another door, and after a few minutes, by trying hard, it was possible to feel something resembling a faint draught.

'That's all I can do for you, gentlemen.'

At last, at eleven o'clock, sounds started to come from behind Maigret's door. Lucas was the first to come out, shepherding the unknown man, who was still holding his hat in front of his face. Lognon brought up the rear. All three walked towards the stairs which connected the Police Judiciaire to the Palais de Justice and then to the underground cells known as the Mousetrap.

The photographers jostled each other. Flash bulbs went off in the corridor. Less than a minute later, the glass door closed, and everyone rushed towards Maigret's office, which looked like the scene of a battlefield. Beer glasses littered the desks, cigarette ends and torn papers were strewn everywhere, and the air smelled of tobacco, now stale. Maigret himself, still jacketless, was leaning into the closet, and washing his hands at the little enamel basin.

'Can you give us some pointers, chief inspector?'

He looked at them with the wide-eyed expression he always wore in these circumstances, appearing not to recognize anyone.

'Pointers?' he repeated.

'Who is he?'

'Who?'

'The man who just left here.'

'Someone with whom I have had a rather long conversation.'

'A witness?'

'No comment.'

'Have you taken him into custody?'

Maigret seemed to wake up a bit, and apologized in an amiable way:

'Gentlemen, I'm sorry not to be able to give you any answers, but frankly, I can't make any statement at this stage.'

'Will you be making one shortly?'

'I don't know.'

'Are you going to see the examining magistrate?'

'Not tonight.'

'Is it to do with the killer?'

'Once more, you will have to forgive me, but I can't give you any information.'

'Are you going home now?'

'What time is it?'

'Half past eleven.'

'In that case, the Brasserie Dauphine is still open, so I'm going for a bite to eat.'

They watched as Maigret, Janvier and Lapointe all left.

Two or three journalists followed them as far as the bar and stood at the counter drinking, while the three police officers, looking tired and concerned, sat down at a table in the back room and gave their orders to the waiter.

A few minutes later, Lognon joined them, but not Lucas. The four men were talking in low voices and it was impossible to hear what they were saying or to guess anything from their lip movements.

'Better call it a day. Want me to take you home, Maguy?'

'No, take me to the paper.'

Once the door had closed behind them, and only then, Maigret stretched. A merry, youthful smile appeared on his lips.

'That's it, then!' he sighed.

Janvier said:

'I think they've swallowed it.'

'Well, I should damn well hope so!'

'What will they write?'

'No idea, but they'll manage to make it sound sensational. Especially that young Rougin.'

He was a new recruit to journalism, young and aggressive.

'What if they realize they've been tricked?'

'It's essential they don't!'

It was an almost entirely different Lognon who was eating with them, a Lognon who since four that afternoon had drunk four glasses of beer, and was not refusing the shot of spirits the café owner came to offer them.

'So how's your wife getting on, Lognon?'

'She's written to say the treatment's going well. She's just worrying about me.'

It didn't make them laugh or even smile. Some subjects are sacrosanct. It did not prevent him being relaxed, almost optimistic.

'You played your role very well. Thank you for that. I hope that apart from Alfonsi, nobody in your station knows anything about this.'

'No, nobody.'

It was half past midnight when they separated. There were still customers sitting out on café terraces, and more people than usual on the streets, breathing in the comparative coolness of the night air, since there had been none during the day.

'You're taking the bus?'

Maigret shook his head. He preferred to make his way home on foot, alone, and as he trod the pavements, his excitement dropped away and a more serious, almost anguished expression took over his face.

If, as happened a few times, he passed a woman hurrying down the street alone, she would invariably be keeping close to the walls, and would shrink back, ready to run or shout for help at the slightest move on his part.

Over the past six months, five women who, like these, had been on their way home or to see a friend, five women on foot in the streets of Paris, had been the victims of the same murderer.

Strangely enough, all five crimes had been committed in just one of Paris' twenty arrondissements, the 18th, Montmartre, and not only the same arrondissement but the same part of it, a very specific area which could be described as being between four Métro stations: Lamarck, Abbesses, Place Blanche and Place Clichy.

The names of the victims, the neighbourhood where the attacks had taken place and the time of each crime had become familiar to newspaper readers, and Maigret was literally haunted by them. He knew the list by heart and could have recited it, like a La Fontaine fable learned at school.

2 February. Avenue Rachel, near Place Clichy, and hardly any distance from Boulevard de Clichy with its bright lights: Arlette Dutour, 28, a streetwalker, living in furnished rooms in Rue d'Amsterdam.

Two stab wounds in the back, one of which had killed her almost instantly. Her clothing had been systematically slashed, and there were a few superficial cuts to her body.

No sign of rape. Neither her jewellery, which was of little value, nor her handbag containing a certain amount of money had been taken.

3 March. Rue Lepic, a little beyond the Moulin de la Galette. 8.15 at night. Joséphine Simmer, born in Mulhouse, a midwife, aged 43. She lived in Rue Lamarck and was on her way back from the top of the Butte Montmartre, where she had been delivering a baby.

A single stab wound in the back, which had penetrated the heart. Clothing slashed, superficial cuts to the body. Her midwife's bag was lying beside her on the pavement.

17 April. (Because of the coincidences of the dates 2 February and 3 March, the police had been expecting another attack on 4 April, but nothing had happened.) Rue Étex, alongside the Montmartre cemetery, almost opposite the Bretonneau hospital. Three minutes past nine at night, Monique Juteaux, a dressmaker, aged 24, unmarried, living with her mother, Boulevard des Batignolles. She was coming back from visiting a friend who lived in Avenue de Saint-Ouen. It was raining, and she had been carrying an umbrella.

Three stab wounds. Clothing slashed, nothing stolen.

15 June. Between 9.20 and 9.30. Rue Durantin this time, still in the same district. Marie Bernard, a widow aged 52, who worked as a post office clerk and lived with her daughter and son-in-law in a flat on Boulevard Rochechouart.

Two stab wounds. Clothing slashed. The second thrust had severed the carotid artery. Nothing stolen.

21 July. The most recent crime so far. Georgette Lecoeur, aged 31, married with two children, living in Rue Lepic, not far from where the second attack had taken place. Her husband worked nights in a garage. One of the children was ill. She was going down Rue Tholozé in search of a chemist's shop open at that time of night, and she had died at about 9.45, opposite a music hall. A single stab wound. Clothing slashed.

It was hideous and monotonous.

Police reinforcements had been posted in the area where the crimes had occurred, known as the Grandes-Carrières. Lognon had, like his colleagues, postponed his holiday leave. Would he ever be able to take it?

The streets were being patrolled. Officers had been stationed at all the strategic points. They had already been in position when the second, third, fourth and fifth murders had taken place.

'Tired?' asked Madame Maigret, as she opened the door of their apartment at exactly the moment her husband reached the landing.

'It was a hot day.'

'Still nothing?'

'Nothing.'

'I heard just now on the radio that there had been some excitement at Quai des Orfèvres.'

'Already?'

'They seemed to think it was to do with the murders in the 18th? Is that true?'

'More or less.'

'Have you got any leads?'

'Not that I know.'

'Did you have any dinner?'

'Yes, and I even had a bite of supper only half an hour ago.'

She didn't insist, and soon afterwards both of them were asleep, with the bedroom window wide open.

He arrived next morning at his office without having had time to read the newspapers. They had been placed on his blotter, and he was about to look at them when the telephone rang. From the first syllable, he recognized who was on the line.

'Maigret?'

'Yes, sir, good morning.'

Coméliau, of course, the examining magistrate in charge of the inquiry into the five crimes in Montmartre.

'Is all this true?'

'What do you mean?'

'What all the papers are saying this morning.'

'I haven't seen them yet.'

'Have you arrested anyone?'

'Not to my knowledge.'

'Perhaps it would be best if you were to come to my office right away.'

'Of course, sir.'

Lucas, who had come into the room and overheard the conversation, understood the expression on Maigret's face.

'Lucas, tell the chief I've gone over to the Palais de Justice and probably won't be back in time for the daily report.'

And Maigret set off in the same direction taken the previous day by Lognon, Lucas and the mysterious visitor, the man whose hat had been hiding his face. In the corridor where the magistrates had their offices, the gendarmes saluted him, while some of those waiting there, witnesses or people called in for questioning, recognized him, and one or two made a sign of greeting.

'Come in! Read this!'

He had been expecting this, of course, that Coméliau would be jumpy and aggressive, and would be restraining with some difficulty the indignation that was making his little moustache quiver.

One headline read:

Have the police nabbed the killer at last?

Another:

Almighty commotion at Police Headquarters!
Is this the Montmartre maniac?

'I would observe to you, detective chief inspector, that yesterday at four o'clock, I was sitting here in my office, less than two hundred metres from yours, with a telephone on my desk. I was still here at five, and at six, and I left for another engagement only at ten to seven. Even then, I could have been reached, whether at home, where you have often called me, or later at the home of some friends, whose address I took care to leave with my manservant.'

Maigret, who had remained on his feet, heard all this without reacting.

'When an event as important as this . . .'

Looking up, Maigret said quietly:

'There hasn't been any event.'

Coméliau, who was already launched so far into his speech that he could not immediately calm down, rapped the newspapers with his clenched fist.

'And all this? Are you going to tell me this has all been invented by the journalists?'

'It's mere speculation on their part.'

19

'In other words, nothing whatsoever happened, and these gentlemen *speculated* that you had an unknown man brought to your office, interrogated him for six hours, then sent him down to the Mousetrap and . . .'

'I didn't interrogate anyone, sir.'

This time Coméliau, taken aback, looked at him in complete incomprehension.

'I think you had better explain yourself to me, so that I can provide some account to the public prosecutor, whose first action this morning was to call my office.'

'A certain person did indeed come to see me yesterday afternoon, along with two inspectors.'

'A person whom the two inspectors had arrested?'

'It was in the nature of a friendly visit.'

'And that was why the man was hiding his face with his hat?'

Coméliau pointed to a photograph printed across two columns of the front pages of the newspapers.

'Perhaps that was mere chance, an automatic movement on his part. We had a chat—'

'For six hours?'

'Time passes quickly.'

'And you had beer and sandwiches sent up?'

'That is quite true, sir.'

The magistrate once more slapped his hand down on the newspapers.

'I have in front of me a detailed account of all your comings and goings.'

'I am sure that is correct.'

'Who is this man?'

'He's a likeable fellow by the name of Mazet, Pierre Mazet, who worked in my squad for a while about ten years ago, just after passing his exams. Later, hoping for faster promotion and also, I believe, because of some unhappy love affair, he asked to be posted to Equatorial Africa, where he stayed for five years.'

Coméliau could make no sense of this and frowned at Maigret, wondering whether the chief inspector was mocking him.

'He had to leave Africa after an attack of fever, and the doctors have forbidden him to return. When he's fully restored to health, he will probably apply to be re-employed at the Police Judiciaire.'

'And it was to receive this man that you created what the newspapers have not hesitated to call an almighty commotion?'

Maigret moved towards the door, to check that nobody could be listening to their conversation.

'Yes, sir, that's right,' he finally admitted. 'I needed a man whose appearance was as ordinary and non-distinctive as possible, and whose face was not known to the press or the general public. Poor Mazet has changed a lot since his spell in Africa. Do you see what I'm getting at?'

'I can't say that I do.'

'I didn't tell the reporters anything. I didn't say a single word to entitle them to think his visit had anything to do with the Montmartre murders.'

'But you didn't deny it either.'

'I repeated that I had nothing to say, which was the truth.'

'And the result . . . !' cried the magistrate, pointing to the papers again.

'The result was the one I wanted to obtain.'

'Without consulting me, of course. Or even keeping me informed!'

'That was entirely so as to spare you from sharing any of the responsibility, sir, it was all mine.'

'What are you hoping to achieve?'

Maigret, whose pipe had gone out, relit it with a thoughtful expression and then said slowly:

'I don't quite know yet. I simply thought that it would be worth trying something.'

Coméliau was still puzzled, and he stared at Maigret's pipe, to which he had never been able to accustom himself. The chief inspector was in fact the only person who ventured to smoke in his office, and the magistrate considered this a kind of provocation.

'Sit down,' he said in the end, regretfully.

And before sitting down himself, he went to open the window.

2. Professor Tissot's Theories

It was on the previous Friday evening that Maigret and his wife had set off walking peaceably towards Rue Picpus, to pay a neighbourly visit: in all the nearby streets, people were sitting in their doorways, and many had even brought chairs out on to the pavement. The Maigrets' regular practice of dining once a month with Doctor Pardon had continued, with a slight variation, introduced about a year ago.

Pardon had taken to inviting, along with the Maigret couple, one or other of his medical colleagues, almost always an interesting man, either in personality or because of his research, and the inspector often found himself sitting opposite the head of a leading medical institution or some illustrious professor.

He had not at first realized that it was these people who had asked to meet *him*, and who were studying him, asking countless questions. All of them had heard of him by reputation and were curious to make his acquaintance. It had not taken long for them to feel that they had some common ground with Maigret, and some of their after-dinner conversations, aided by a well-aged liqueur in the Pardons' peaceful sitting room, usually with the windows open on to the busy street, had lasted late into the night.

Many times, following one of these chats, Maigret's opposite number would suddenly ask him with a serious expression:

'And you were never tempted to go in for medicine?'

He would answer, almost with a blush, that such had indeed been his first intention, but that his father's death had obliged him to give up his studies.

It was curious, was it not, that they could sense this after so many years? Their interest in human behaviour, with its troubles and its failings, was almost identical with his own.

And the policeman did not try to conceal that he was flattered that these professors, often household names, were drawn to talk shop with him almost as if they were colleagues.

Had Doctor Pardon planned this deliberately that night, on account of the Montmartre killer, whose crimes had been preoccupying all of Paris for months? It was possible. Pardon was an unpretentious man, certainly, but capable of great tact and subtlety. This year, he had had to take his holiday early, in June, since that was the only time for which he could find a locum.

When Maigret and his wife arrived, another couple was already in the living room with the tray of aperitifs: the man was of sturdy peasant build, with a ruddy complexion and thick, grey, crew-cut hair; his wife was dark and extremely vivacious.

Doctor Pardon introduced them: 'My friends the Maigrets . . . Madame Tissot . . . and Professor Tissot.'

This was the famous Tissot, director of the Sainte-Anne

Psychiatric Institution in Rue Cabanis. Although the professor was often called upon as an expert witness in court, Maigret had never had occasion to meet him, and he found himself faced with a solid, humane and jovial psychiatrist, of a kind he had not before encountered.

They soon moved to the dinner table. It was still hot outside, but towards the end of the meal a fine rain began to fall, and its sound, audible through the open windows, was the accompaniment to the rest of the evening.

Professor Tissot was not taking a holiday because, although he owned an apartment in Paris, he returned almost every evening to his country property in Ville d'Avray, south-west of the capital.

Like previous guests, he began, while talking of this and that, to observe the inspector with rapid glances, as if each impression added another touch to the image he was forming of him. It was once they had retired to the drawing room, and the women had grouped themselves spontaneously in a corner, that he made a direct inquiry:

'Does your responsibility not terrify you a little?'

Maigret understood at once: 'I presume you're referring to the murders in Montmartre.'

His interlocutor blinked agreement. And it was true that, for Maigret, this case was one of the most distressing in his career. It was not simply a matter of the police finding the murderer. And for society in general, it was not, as it normally would be, a question of punishing the killer.

It was a matter of defence. Five women had died, and there was no reason to think it would stop there.

Yet the normal defence mechanisms were not working. If proof were needed, it was that immediately after the first murder a large-scale police operation had been launched, but it had failed to prevent the subsequent attacks.

Maigret believed he could see what Tissot meant when he spoke of his responsibility. It was upon him, or rather upon *his approach to the problem*, that the fate of a certain number of women depended.

Had Pardon felt conscious of this as well, and was that the reason for his arranging this meeting?

'Although it is in a sense my area of expertise,' Tissot had added, 'I wouldn't care to be in your position, with the public panicking, the press doing nothing to reassure people, and the authorities calling for contradictory measures in response. Am I right?'

'Yes, indeed.'

'I assume you have noted the characteristic features of the different crimes?'

He was getting directly to the heart of the matter, and Maigret might have thought he was talking to one of his colleagues at the Police Judiciaire.

'May I ask, between ourselves, what has struck you most about them?'

This was almost like being asked an examination question, and Maigret, to whom this seldom happened, felt himself colouring.

'The type of victim,' he replied however, without hesitation. 'You are asking about the principal feature, I take it? I haven't told you about the others, which are quite numerous.

'When, as in this case, we have a series of crimes, our first concern at Quai des Orfèvres is to look for points they have in common.'

Tissot, a glass of Armagnac in his hand, nodded approval: the dinner had brought high colour to his cheeks.

'The time of day, for example?' he asked.

It was easy to guess his desire to show that he knew about the case, that he too, by reading the press reports, had studied it from every angle, including that of the police investigation.

It was Maigret's turn to smile, since this was quite touching.

'Yes, indeed, the time of day. The first attack took place at eight in the evening, in February. At that time of year, it was dark. The crime on the 3rd of March was a quarter of an hour later, and so on with the other murders, ending in July, with an attack a little before ten o'clock. Evidently, the killer was waiting for darkness to fall.'

'And the dates?'

'I've studied them twenty times, until they're going round and round in my head. In my office, you'd find a calendar covered in notes in blue, black and red ink. As if I were trying to decipher some secret language, and I have tried every system and code I could think of. Some people wondered at first whether it was anything to do with the full moon.'

'People do tend to attach a lot of importance to the

moon when something happens that they can't understand.'

'What about you?'

'Speaking as a doctor, no.'

'And as a man?'

'I don't know.'

'It doesn't seem to apply here, at any rate, because only two of the attacks took place on nights when the moon was full. So I tried other approaches. The day of the week, for instance. Some people get drunk on Saturday nights. But only one of the crimes was committed on a Saturday. And there are certain occupations where the day off isn't Sunday, but some other day.'

Maigret had the feeling that Tissot had, like him, envisaged all these different hypotheses.

'The first constant, if I can call it that, which we identified was the district of Paris, the neighbourhood west of Montmartre. It's clear that the murderer knows this like the back of his hand. It's as a result of this knowledge of the streets, the places that are well lit or not, and the distances between any two given points, that he has managed not only not to be caught, but even to avoid being seen.'

'The papers have mentioned witnesses who claim to have seen him.'

'We took statements from them all. The woman who lives on the first floor in Avenue Rachel, for instance, the one who was most categorical, claims the man was tall and thin, wearing a cream-coloured raincoat and a felt hat pulled down over his eyes. In the first place, that sounds like a very standard description, the kind you get too many of in cases like this, and at Quai des Orfèvres we tend not to trust them. And in any case, from the window where this woman says she was standing, it's impossible to see the place she meant.

'As for the statement from the little boy, that was more convincing, but so vague it can't be used – it was about the attack in Rue Durantin, remember that?'

Tissot nodded.

'So, in short, this man knows the local streets very well indeed, and that's why people imagine he lives there, which has created a particularly distressing atmosphere locally. Everyone is watching the neighbours with suspicion. We've received hundreds of letters informing us about the strange behaviour of perfectly normal people.

'We tried thinking in terms of a man who might not *live* in the neighbourhood, but who might work there.'

'That sounds very time-consuming.'

'Thousands of man-hours. Not to mention going through our files, checking and updating our lists of known criminals and maniacs. You must have received, like the other hospitals, a questionnaire about any patients discharged in recent years.'

'Yes, my colleagues sent in our reply.'

'The same questionnaire was sent to mental hospitals all over France and even abroad, and to doctors who might have treated such patients.'

'You suggested there was some other constant.'

'You will have seen the photographs of the victims in

the papers. They were published at different dates, obviously. I don't know whether you had the curiosity to line them up side by side?'

Tissot nodded again.

'These women came from different backgrounds – geographically in the first place. One of them was born in Mulhouse in Alsace, another in the south of France, another in Brittany, and the other two in either Paris or the suburbs.

'From the point of view of occupation, there is nothing to connect them: a prostitute, a midwife, a dressmaker, a post-office worker and a full-time mother.

'They didn't all live in the local area.

'We've established that these women did not know each other, and it is more than probable that they had never even met.'

'I hadn't realized that you conducted your inquiries from such varying perspectives.'

'We went further than that. We checked, for example, whether they might have worshipped at the same church, or shopped at the same butcher's, that they weren't patients of the same doctor or dentist, that they didn't happen to go on a particular day of the week to the cinema or perhaps to a dance hall. So when I say thousands of man-hours . . .'

'And all this has yielded no result?'

'Nothing. In fact, I wasn't really expecting that it would, but I was obliged to do the checks. We can't let even the slightest possibility be overlooked.'

'Did you think about holidays?'

'I know what you mean. They might all have taken their holidays in the same resort, in the country or by the sea, but no, it wasn't the case.'

'So it seems that the murderer picked them by chance, just as the occasion presented itself.'

Maigret was sure that Professor Tissot did not believe this, and that he had in fact noticed the same thing as himself.

'No. Not entirely. These women, as I suggested, if you look carefully at their photographs, do have something in common: none of them is thin. If you don't look at their faces, but pay attention to their build, you will see that they are all quite short and rather plump, even running to fat, with thick waists and generous hips, even Monique Juteaux, the youngest of them.'

Pardon and the professor exchanged glances, and it was as if Pardon was saying 'I told you so, didn't I? He spotted it too.'

Tissot smiled.

'My compliments, my dear chief inspector, I see that you have nothing to learn from me.'

He added, after a brief hesitation:

'I did mention something about this to Pardon, wondering whether the police had noticed it. It was in part because of that, but also because I had been keen to meet you for a long time, that he invited my wife and me here tonight.'

The men had been standing up all this while. Their host suggested they go and sit in a corner by the window overlooking Rue Picpus, from which they could hear the distant sounds of radio sets. The rain was still falling, but it was so fine that the drops seemed to be alighting delicately on top of each other, to form a sort of dark lacquer on the cobblestones.

Maigret broke the silence.

'Do you know, professor, the question that troubles me most, the one that would, in my view, help us lay hands on the killer, if we could only answer it?'

'I'm listening.'

'This man is not a child any longer. He's lived for a number of years – twenty, thirty, maybe more – without committing any crime. And then in the space of six months, he has killed five times. The question I ask myself is, how did this start? *Why*, on the 2nd of February, did he suddenly stop being an inoffensive citizen, and turn into a dangerous maniac? You're a man of science, do you see any explanation?'

This made Tissot smile and once more he glanced across at his medical colleague.

'We men of science, as you call us, are readily assumed to have knowledge and powers that we don't possess. But I'm going to try and give you an answer, concerning not only the initial shock but the case in itself.

'And I'm not going to use any particular scientific or technical jargon, because that often only masks our ignorance. Don't you agree, Pardon?'

He must have been alluding to colleagues towards whom he felt some animosity, since the two medical men seemed to understand one another.

'Faced with a series of crimes like the one we're talking about, most people will react by assuming that it must be the work of a maniac, a madman. And by and large, that is true. To kill five women in the circumstances surrounding these five murders, for no apparent reason, and then to lacerate their garments, certainly does not correspond to the behaviour of a normal man as we would think of it.

'As for being able to determine why and how it began, that's an extremely complex question, to which it is hard to give an answer.

'Almost every week, I'm called on to testify as an expert witness at the Assizes. In the course of my career, I have seen the definition of responsibility in criminal matters change so rapidly that, in my view, all our conceptions of justice have been altered, if not overturned.

'We used to be asked:

'"At the time of the crime, was the accused responsible for his actions?"

'And the word "responsible" had a fairly clear meaning.

'Nowadays, it is the responsibility of Man, with a capital M, that we're being asked to evaluate, to the point where I often get the impression that it isn't the jury or the judges who decide the fate of a criminal, but us, the psychiatrists.

'Yet in most cases, we know no more than a layman would.

'Psychiatry can be described as a science when there is some trauma, say, or a tumour, or an abnormal transformation of a gland or a function.

'In cases like that, we can state in all conscience whether a given man is either healthy or sick, responsible for his actions or not.

'But those are the rarest of cases, and most of such individuals are already in institutions.

'So why do some *other* people, such probably as the one we're talking about, do things differently from their fellow men?

'I think, chief inspector, that in those cases, you know as much if not more than we do.'

Madame Pardon had come over to them, carrying the bottle of Armagnac.

'Don't let me interrupt you, gentlemen. We are exchanging recipes. A little Armagnac, professor?'

'Just a drop.'

They carried on chatting in the evening twilight, which was as soft as the rain falling outside, until past one in the morning. Maigret could not later remember all of their conversation, which had often veered on to parallel topics.

He did remember that Tissot had said, with the irony of a man who has an old score to settle:

'If I subscribed blindly to the theories of Freud or Adler, or even today's psychoanalysts, I wouldn't hesitate to say that our man is a sexual maniac, even though none of his victims was attacked sexually . . .

'I could talk about complexes too, and impressions formed in early childhood.'

'And you would reject such an explanation?'

'I wouldn't reject anything, but I distrust glib solutions.'

'And you don't have a personal theory?'

'Theory, no. An idea perhaps, but I'm a little afraid, I confess, to mention it to you, because you carry responsibility for the investigation on your shoulders. It's true that your shoulders are as broad as mine. Son of a farmer?'

'From the Allier.'

'I'm from the Cantal. My father's eighty-eight and still lives on his farm.'

And anyone would have sworn that the professor was prouder of that than of his scientific qualifications.

'I have had pass through my hands many deranged or perhaps semi-deranged people, if I can use an unscientific expression, who have committed criminal acts, and if there is a constant, to use your own word just now, it is one that I have always identified in them: a conscious or unconscious need to assert themselves. Do you see what I mean by that?'

Maigret nodded his assent.

'Almost all of them have been regarded by those around them, rightly or wrongly, as spineless, mediocre or incompetent individuals, and they have felt humiliated by that. What is the mechanism that makes this long-repressed humiliation suddenly burst out, in the form of a crime, an attack or some gesture of defiance or bravado? Neither I, nor I think my colleagues, have been able to establish that with any certainty.

'What I'm saying now isn't orthodox opinion, especially when put very briefly, but I am convinced that so-called motiveless crimes are above all a display of pride.'

Maigret looked thoughtful.

'That fits with something I've noticed,' he murmured.

'And that is?'

'That if criminals did not feel the need, sooner or later,

to boast of their acts, there would be a great many fewer of them in prison. Do you know where we look first for the suspect, after the kind of crime we describe as squalid? In the old days it was in the brothels; now that they have been abolished we have to question streetwalkers. Because the men talk! They're sure that with such women they are safe, it doesn't matter, they're not risking anything, which is in most cases true. They describe their crimes, sometimes with embellishments.'

'Have you tried that lead this time?'

'Over the last few months, we've approached all the prostitutes in Paris, especially in the Clichy–Montmartre neighbourhood.'

'And that hasn't produced anything?'

'No.'

'Then it's worse.'

'You mean that, not having been able to get it off his chest, he's bound to start again?'

'I'd be inclined to think so.'

Maigret had in recent days been studying historical examples with analogies to the Montmartre case, from Jack the Ripper to the Düsseldorf Vampire, by way of the Lamplighter of Vienna, and the homicidal Polish farmer in the French *département* of Aisne.

'Do you think that such men would ever stop of their own accord?' he asked. 'Still, there is the example of Jack the Ripper, who stopped committing murders almost overnight.'

'What evidence is there that he wasn't himself the victim of an accident, or died of some disease? I'd go further than that, inspector, and here it's not the director of Sainte-Anne talking, because I'm going to leave official theories a long way behind.

'Individuals of the kind you're after are driven, unconsciously, by the need to be caught, and that's another form of pride. They can't stand the idea that people around them should continue to think of them as quite ordinary, humdrum individuals. They have to be able to shout out loud to the whole world what they've done, what they're capable of.

'It doesn't mean that they allow themselves to be caught deliberately, but, almost always, they take fewer and fewer precautions as their crimes mount up, in a way that seems to be taunting the police, tempting fate.

'Such men have confessed to me that it was actually a relief to be arrested at last,' Tissot added.

'I have heard similar confessions.'

'There you are!'

Whose idea had it been? They had been sitting so long that evening, discussing the subject from so many angles, that afterwards it was difficult to establish who had said what.

Perhaps the suggestion had been put forward by Tissot, but so discreetly that even Pardon did not notice.

It was already past midnight when Maigret had murmured, as if talking to himself:

'Just supposing someone *else* were to be arrested, and in a way take the place of our killer, usurping what he thinks is his personal fame?'

They had reached a turning point in their discussion.

'I think in that case,' Tissot replied, 'your man would indeed feel a degree of frustration.

'But it would remain to be seen how he'd react. And *when* he'd react.'

Maigret was already ahead of them, abandoning theory to envisage practical solutions.

They knew nothing about the murderer. They had no description of him. Until now, he had been operating in a particular area of Paris, but nothing proved that he would not strike again in another district of the capital, or somewhere else entirely.

What made this threat so distressing was that it was so vague and imprecise.

Would it be a month before his next crime? Or only three days?

They could not keep every street in Paris in a state of siege indefinitely. Parisian women themselves, who after each murder had, as it were, taken cover, would soon return to their normal lives and risk venturing out at night, telling themselves the danger was over.

'I know of two cases,' Maigret went on after a short silence, 'where a criminal actually wrote to the newpapers to protest about the arrest of an innocent party.'

'That kind of person often writes to the papers, under compulsion from what I would call their exhibitionism.'

'It would help us.'

Even a letter made up of words cut out of newspapers could become a lead, in an investigation where they had nothing solid to go on.

'Obviously, there's another possible response he might make.'

'The same thought has occurred to me.'

A very simple response: if the wrong culprit was arrested, the killer might immediately commit another murder like the first ones! Or perhaps two or three more.

They parted on the pavement, standing by the professor's car, since he and his wife were returning to Ville d'Avray.

'May I offer you a lift home?'

'No, we live nearby, and we're used to the walk.'

'I have a feeling that this case may well bring me once again to act as expert witness in court.'

'That's if I can lay hands on the culprit.'

'I have every confidence in you.'

They shook hands and Maigret sensed that it was the beginning of a friendship.

'You didn't get a chance to speak to *her*,' remarked Madame Maigret a little later, as they were walking home. 'That's a pity, because she's the most intelligent woman I've ever met. What's her husband like?'

'Very impressive.'

She pretended not to see what Maigret was up to surreptitiously, something he had done as a child. The rain was so cool and delicious that from time to time he was sticking his tongue out to catch a few drops, which had a special taste.

'You seemed to be having a serious discussion.'

'Yes . . .'

And that was all that was said on the subject. Back at their apartment, the windows had been left open and Madame Maigret had to wipe up a little water from the parquet floor.

Perhaps it was as he dropped off to sleep, or else on waking next morning, that Maigret took his decision. And by complete chance, it was in the course of that morning that his former inspector, Pierre Mazet, whom he had not seen for eight years, turned up in his office.

'What are you doing in Paris?'

'Nothing, boss. I'm convalescing. The African mosquitoes have done me some damage, and the doctors insist I should take a few more months' rest. After that, I was wondering whether there might be some small job for me at headquarters.'

'Well now!'

Why not Mazet? He was intelligent, and there was little risk he would be recognized.

'Would you like to help me out with something?'

'Are you asking *me* that, boss!'

'Come and see me about twelve thirty, and we'll go for lunch.'

Not at the Brasserie Dauphine, where they would not pass unnoticed.

'No, in fact don't come back here at all, and don't do the rounds of the offices, but wait for me outside Châtelet Métro station.'

They lunched at a restaurant in Rue Saint-Antoine, on the right bank, and the inspector explained to Mazet what he wanted him to do.

To make it look convincing, it would be best if he was not brought into the Police Judiciaire by anyone from Quai des Orfèvres, but by some inspectors from the 18th arrondissement, and Maigret had immediately thought of

Lognon. Who knows? It might even give him a bit of an opportunity. Instead of patrolling the streets of Montmartre, he would be involved more closely in the investigation.

'Choose one of your colleagues who can keep his mouth shut.'

Lognon had chosen Alfonsi.

And they had played out their little drama with great success as far as the press was concerned, since all the papers were already talking about a 'sensational arrest'.

And now, as Maigret repeated to Coméliau:

'The reporters were present throughout certain comings and goings, and they drew their own conclusions. Neither I nor any of my colleagues told them anything. On the contrary, we denied everything.'

It was unusual to see a smile, even a sarcastic one, on the magistrate's face.

'And what if tonight or tomorrow people stop taking precautions because of this arrest – or rather false arrest – and another crime is committed?'

'I've thought of that. Firstly, for the next few nights, all the available officers from our service and the 18th arrondissement will be patrolling the district carefully.'

'That's already been done, but without success, it seems to me.'

This was true. But did that mean they shouldn't try anything?

'I took another precaution. I went to see the prefect of police.'

'Without telling me?'

'As I said, I intend to take full responsibility for anything that might happen. I'm merely a policeman, you're a magistrate.'

This reply pleased Coméliau, who instantly adopted a more dignified attitude.

'What did you ask the prefect?'

'Permission to use as volunteers a certain number of women police officers from the municipal force.'

The auxiliary corps of women police officers usually handled only matters dealing with children or prostitution.

'He has recruited a certain number who correspond to a particular profile.'

'For example?'

'Height and weight. I chose, from among the volunteers, the ones who most closely resemble the physical build of the five victims. And like the victims, they will be inconspicuously dressed. They will act as if they are local women, just going from one place to another in their district, and some of them will be carrying a parcel or a shopping bag.'

'So in sum, you are setting a trap?'

'All the women I have chosen have been on physical training courses and they have also been to judo classes.'

Coméliau nevertheless looked nervous.

'Should I tell the public prosecutor about this?'

'Better not.'

'You know, chief inspector, I don't like this at all.'

And Maigret, with disarming frankness, replied:

'Neither do I, sir.'

It was true.

But should they not try every possible means of preventing the slaughter continuing?

'Officially, I haven't been informed about this, then?' said the magistrate, seeing Maigret to the door.

'You know absolutely nothing about it.'

Maigret would have preferred it if that were true.

3. A Neighbourhood under Siege

The Baron, who as a reporter had frequented the Police Judiciaire almost as long as Maigret, accompanied by Rougin – younger but already sharper than his colleagues – plus five or six other less notable journalists, including Maguy (the most dangerous since she did not hesitate, with an air of innocence, to push open doors carelessly left unlocked, or to pick up papers left lying around), and one or two photographers, a few more at times, spent a good part of the day in the corridor at Quai des Orfèvres, which they had made their headquarters.

Sometimes the greater part of the press crew would disappear to take refreshment at the Brasserie Dauphine, or to make telephone calls, but they always left someone on duty, so that the door to Maigret's office was never left unwatched.

Rougin had also had the idea of getting someone from his newspaper to shadow Inspector Lognon, who was thus being followed from the moment he stepped outside his home on Place Constantin-Pecqueur in the morning.

All these journalists knew the score, as they would put it, and had almost as much experience of police matters as a senior inspector.

And yet not one of them suspected the deception that was taking place almost before their eyes, a kind of gigantic theatrical performance which had begun in the early hours, well before Maigret's visit to the examining magistrate.

For example, inspectors normally stationed in more distant arrondissements like the 12th, 14th or 15th, had left home wearing different clothes from usual, some of them with suitcases or even a trunk, and they had taken care, following instructions, to make their first port of call one of the capital's railway stations.

The heat was almost as oppressive as on the previous day, and life had slowed down, except in the tourist districts, where the ubiquitous buses laden with foreign sightseers were driving around, the voices of their guides audible in the streets.

In the 18th arrondissement, and especially in the area within which the five crimes had been committed, taxis were stopping in front of hotels and furnished tenements, and people were getting out of them as if arriving from the provinces and needing rooms, almost always insisting that they should have a view of the street.

All this was taking place according to a precise plan, and some of the inspectors had received orders to have their wives accompany them.

It was only rarely that such arrangements were set in motion. But in this case, could anyone be trusted? Nothing was known about the killer. That was another aspect of the question that Professor Tissot and Maigret had discussed during their evening at the Pardons'.

'So in short, apart from these crises, he must of necessity behave quite normally, otherwise his oddities would have attracted the attention of those around him?'

'Of necessity, as you say,' the psychiatrist had agreed. 'It's even probable that in his appearance, his behaviour and his occupation, this is the kind of person who would arouse the very *least* suspicion.'

He could not be a habitual sex offender, because these were already known, and since the 2nd of February they had been kept under observation, but without result. Nor could he be one of the wretched vagrants or disquieting individuals whom one turns to look at in the street because of their strange behaviour.

What had he been doing before his first crime? What did he do in the intervals between the murders?

Was he a solitary individual, living in rented lodgings, or a furnished room? Maigret would have been prepared to lay money that no, this would be a married man, leading a regular life, and Tissot too inclined to that hypothesis.

'Anything's possible,' the professor had said with a sigh. 'You could tell me he was one of my own colleagues, and I wouldn't protest. It could be anyone, a workman, a clerk, a shopkeeper or an important businessman.'

He might also be one of the managers of the hotels on which the police inspectors were descending en masse, which was why they could not simply turn up at the front desk, as they usually did, and announce:

'Police! Give me a room with a view on the street, and not a word to anyone!'

Nor could they entirely trust the local concierges. Nor their usual informers in the Montmartre district.

When Maigret returned to his office after leaving

Coméliau, he was besieged by reporters, as he had been the day before.

'Have you been conferring with the examining magistrate?'

'I went to see him, as I do every morning.'

'Did you tell him about the person you questioned yesterday?'

'We talked about this and that.'

'You still won't tell us anything?'

'I've no comment to make at present.'

He went in to see the chief. The daily report had been handed in much earlier. The commissioner too looked concerned.

'Coméliau didn't ask you to put a stop to the whole thing?'

'No. Of course, if something goes wrong, he'll let me take the rap.'

'Are you still sure about this?'

'I have to be.'

Maigret was not trying out his experiment with a light heart, and was well aware of the responsibility he was shouldering.

'You really think the reporters will swallow this, hook, line and sinker?'

'I'm doing my utmost to make them.'

Normally, he had a cordial working relationship with the press, which can provide the police with valuable services. But this time, he couldn't take the risk of an involuntary indiscretion. Even the inspectors who were now dispersed all over the Grandes-Carrières neighbourhood were not sure exactly what was being planned. They had received orders to take up position at given points and wait for instructions. They suspected, of course, that it was to do with the murderer, but were not privy to the overall operation.

'Do you think he's intelligent?' Maigret had asked Professor Tissot during their conversation.

He had his own ideas about this; nevertheless he felt he would like to receive confirmation.

'Yes, but it's the kind of intelligence that such people often have. For instance, he must have an instinctive and outstanding talent for playing a role. If we suppose he's married, for example, he has to revert to his normal behaviour, not to mention keeping his sangfroid, when he returns home after committing a crime. If he's unmarried, he must still have to meet other people, if only his landlady, the concierge or the charwoman, that kind of person. Next day, he goes to work in his office, or in a factory, and of course those around him will be talking about the Montmartre murderer. And in all these six months, nobody has suspected him. In six months, he hasn't put a foot wrong with time or place. No witnesses can reliably claim to have seen him in action, or even running away from the scene of the crime.'

That had led to a question which troubled the inspector.

'I'd like your view on a particular point. You just said that most of the time he acts like a normal man, and then, no doubt, he *thinks* like a normal man?'

'I understand what you mean. Yes, probably.'

'Five times, he has had what I would call a crisis, five

times, he has broken out of normality, in order to kill. At what moment did the impulse seize him? Do you see what I mean? At what moment does he stop acting like you or me, and start acting like a killer? Does it strike him at some point during the day, and does he then wait for nightfall to prepare his plan of action? Or on the contrary, does the impulse come over him the instant an opportunity offers itself? At the very moment when, walking down an empty street, he sees a possible victim?'

For Maigret, the answer was of capital importance because it might widen or narrow the field of inquiry. If the impulse struck at the moment of the attack, the killer must live in the Grandes-Carrières neighbourhood, or very close by, or need to be there at night, because of his work or for some other practical reason.

If the opposite was true, it was possible that he could come from anywhere, and have chosen the streets around Place Clichy, Rue Lamarck and Rue des Abbesses because they offered an opportunity, or for some special reason known only to him.

Tissot had reflected for a long while before speaking.

'I can't of course offer a diagnosis, as if I had the patient in front of me . . .'

He had used the word 'patient', as if it concerned one of the people he normally dealt with, and the word, which Maigret did not fail to notice, pleased him. It confirmed that they were both envisaging these events from the same perspective.

'In my view, though, to use a metaphor, there is a moment when he begins the chase, like a wild beast, some big predator, or even a domestic cat. Have you ever watched a cat prowling?'

'Yes, often, in my young days.'

'Its movements are no longer the same. It crouches down, drawing itself in, and all its senses are alerted. It becomes capable of perceiving the slightest sound, or movement, or smell over a considerable distance. And from that moment, it knows how to scent dangers and avoid them.'

'Yes, I see.'

'It's rather as if, once he's in that state, our man is gifted with second sight.'

'There's nothing, I suppose, that allows you to suggest a hypothesis about what could trigger the mechanism?'

'No, not at all. Perhaps a memory, the sight of a woman in the crowd, a whiff of perfume, a sentence overheard. It could be anything, including the sight of a knife, or a dress of a particular colour. Did anyone check the colour of the clothes the victims were wearing? The press didn't mention anything about that.'

'The colours were different, but they were almost all inconspicuous enough not to stand out at night.'

When Maigret returned to his office, he took off his jacket as he had the previous day, removed his tie and opened his shirt collar, then, since the sunlight was striking his armchair, he pulled down the canvas blind. After that, he opened the door to the inspectors' room.

'You there, Janvier?'

'Yes, boss.'

'Anything to report? No anonymous letters?'

'Just letters from people pointing the finger at their neighbours.'

'Check them out. And I want Mazet brought up.'

Mazet had not had to sleep in the cells but had gone home, leaving the Palais de Justice by an unmarked door. He was supposed to be back in the Mousetrap by eight in the morning.

'Shall I go down myself?'

'That would be best.'

'Still no handcuffs?'

'No.'

He did not wish to go to such lengths of deception for the journalists' sake. Let them simply draw their conclusions from what they were seeing. Maigret would not go so far as to deal cheating cards.

'Hello? Get me the station at Grandes-Carrières, please . . . Inspector Lognon . . . Hello! Lognon? Any news your end?'

'Someone was waiting for me this morning outside my front door, and he followed me. He's standing opposite the station now.'

'Not hiding, then?'

'No, I think he's a journalist.'

'Get his papers checked. Everything going as planned?'

'I've located three rooms, belonging to friends. They don't know what it's about. Do you want the addresses?'

'No. Get here in about three quarters of an hour.'

The same scene as before was then re-enacted in the corridor, when Pierre Mazet made his appearance, flanked by two inspectors, once more holding his hat in front of his face. The photographers got to work. The journalists called out questions which were left unanswered. Maguy managed to dislodge the hat which she picked up off the floor, as the ex-colonial policeman hid his face with his hands.

The door closed behind him, and Maigret's office quickly took on the appearance of a command centre.

In the peaceful streets of Montmartre, where many of the small shops were closed for a month or a fortnight because of the summer holidays, the planned scenario was still being silently launched.

Over four hundred people had a part to play, not only the watchers in hotel bedrooms or in the few private apartments made available without risk of indiscretion, but also those who were going to take up set positions outside Métro stations, at bus stops, and in the smallest bistros and restaurants open in the evening.

So that it would not look too much like an invasion, the operation was to proceed in stages.

The policewomen were also receiving detailed instructions by telephone, and as in military headquarters, maps had been spread out, with the location of each person marked.

Twenty inspectors, chosen from those who did not as a rule appear in public, had hired, not only in Paris but in the suburbs, and as far away as Versailles, cars with innocuous number plates, which would be parked at an agreed time in strategic places, where they would not stand out from other vehicles.

'Order some beer up, Lucas.'

'Sandwiches?'

'Yes, you'd better.'

Not only for the benefit of the journalists, to make them think further questioning was taking place, but because they were all busy and no one would have time to go out for lunch.

Lognon arrived in turn, still wearing his red tie and his straw hat. At first sight, the others wondered what had changed about him and they were surprised to realize how much the colour of a necktie can transform a man. He looked quite debonair.

'Did the man follow you?'

'Yes, he's in the corridor now. He is indeed a reporter.'

'Did one of them stay up at your station?'

'One of them's actually *inside* the station.'

An early newspaper edition reported on events at about midday. It repeated the information carried by the morning papers, adding that there was a frenzied atmosphere at Quai des Orfèvres, suggesting major developments afoot, but that total secrecy still surrounded the man who had been arrested.

If the police had been able to, the article remarked, 'the man would no doubt have been issued with an iron mask'.

This amused Mazet. He was helping the others, making phone calls along with them, drawing crosses in red or blue pencil on the street map, very happy to be breathing in the atmosphere of headquarters where he already felt at home again.

The atmosphere changed when the waiter from the Brasserie Dauphine knocked at the door, since even for him it was necessary to put on a show, after which every-one fell on the beer and sandwiches. The afternoon papers carried no message from the murderer, who did not seem to have any intention of contacting the press.

'I'm going to take a nap, boys. Tonight I'll need to be alert and wide awake.'

Maigret crossed the inspectors' large office and went into a small empty room where he settled in an armchair; a few minutes later he had dozed off.

At about three o'clock, he sent Mazet back to the Mouse-trap, and ordered Janvier and Lucas to take it in turns to get some rest. As for Lapointe, he was clad in a workman's blue overalls and driving round the streets of the Grandes-Carrières neighbourhood in a three-wheeled delivery van. Cloth cap aslant on his head, cigarette glued to his lower lip, he looked about eighteen, and from time to time, if he stopped in some café for a white wine and Vichy water, he telephoned headquarters.

As time passed, everyone's nerves became more frayed, and Maigret himself was losing some of his assurance.

There was no indication that anything at all would hap-pen that evening. Even if the man decided to kill again in order to assert himself, it might be the next evening, or the one after that, or in eight, ten days' time, and it would be impossible to keep so many officers on this high level of alert.

It would also be impossible to keep for a whole week a secret that was shared among so many people.

And what if the man decided to act right away?

His conversation with Professor Tissot was still echoing

inside Maigret's head, and snatches of it kept coming back to him.

At what moment would the impulse strike? Just now, while they were all occupied in setting the trap, he would be appearing to anyone he encountered as an ordinary man, like everyone else. People were talking to him, no doubt, serving him food, or shaking his hand. He would be talking too, smiling or laughing perhaps.

Had the trigger already been activated? Had it happened this morning when he read the papers?

Or would he not be more inclined to tell himself that, since the police thought they had the culprit, the investigation would be stood down, and therefore he would be safe.

What proof was there that Tissot and Maigret were on the right track, and that they had correctly judged the reaction of the man the professor had called 'the patient'?

Until now, he had struck only at night-time, waiting for it to be dark. But even at this hour of day, given the holidays and the heat, there were plenty of streets in Paris where several minutes could go by before any passer-by appeared.

Maigret recalled how streets felt in the south of France in summertime, at the siesta hour, the closed shutters and drowsy atmosphere of a whole village or town in the heat of the sun.

Today in Montmartre there were streets almost like that.

The police had however made a certain number of calculations.

At each spot where one of the murders had taken place,

the topography was such that the attacker had been able to disappear within a very short time. Shorter at night than in the daytime, of course. But even in broad daylight, with favourable circumstances, he would still have been able to slash his victim's clothes and make his getaway in under two minutes.

Indeed, did this all necessarily take place in the street? What was there to prevent him knocking at a door where he knew a woman would be alone, and acting in the same way as on the public thoroughfare? Nothing, except that manic individuals, like most criminals – even thieves – *almost always* employ the same method and repeat themselves in the smallest details.

It would be light until about nine o'clock, and not really dark until about nine thirty. The moon, in its third quarter, would not be too bright, and there was a good chance that, as on the previous evening, it would be veiled in cloud because of the heat.

All these details had their importance.

'Are they still out in the corridor?'

'Just the Baron.'

The reporters generally arranged among themselves to leave one person on guard, who would alert the others if anything happened.

'At six o'clock, everyone is to go off as usual, except for Lucas, who will hold the fort here, and Torrence will join him at eight.'

With Janvier, Lognon and Mauvoisin, Maigret went to take an aperitif at the Brasserie Dauphine.

At seven he returned home and sat down to dinner,

looking out through the open window on to Boulevard Richard-Lenoir, calmer now than at any other time of the year.

'You've been feeling the heat!' remarked Madame Maigret, scrutinizing his shirt. 'If you're going out again, you'd better change.'

'I am going out.'

'He hasn't confessed?'

He preferred not to reply, since he disliked lying to her.

'Will you be late back?'

'More than likely.'

'Is there any hope that when this case is over, we might take a holiday?'

During the winter they had talked of going to Brittany, a place called Beuzec-Conq, near Concarneau, but as happened almost every year, their holiday plans had been postponed month after month.

'Possibly,' Maigret sighed.

If not, it would mean that his scheme had failed, and that the killer had slipped through the net, or had not reacted in the way he and Tissot had predicted. It would also mean more victims, exasperation from the public and the press, irony or bad temper from Coméliau and, as happened only too often, questions in the National Assembly and explanations to be delivered in high places.

Above all, it would mean more dead women, short, plump women, looking like ordinary housewives popping out in the evening to go to the shops or visit someone nearby.

'You look tired.'

He was in no hurry to leave. After dinner he loitered in

the apartment, smoking his pipe, wondering whether to have a small glass of plum brandy, and sometimes moving to the window, where finally he stood, leaning on his elbows.

Madame Maigret did not disturb him again. Only, when he made to pick up his jacket, she brought him a clean shirt and helped him on with it. He tried to be as discreet as possible, but she still saw him open a drawer and take out his automatic, which he slipped into his pocket.

This did not happen often. He had no wish to kill anyone, even somebody as dangerous as in this case. Nevertheless, he had ordered all his colleagues to be armed, and to protect the women *at all costs*.

He did not return to Quai des Orfèvres. It was nine o'clock when he arrived at the corner of Boulevard Voltaire, where an unmarked police car was waiting for him with a man at the wheel. The driver, attached to the police station in the 18th arrondissement, was wearing a chauffeur's uniform.

'Where to, sir?'

Maigret took his seat in the back, which was already in shadow as twilight fell, so that the car now looked like one of those which tourists could hire for the day from near the Madeleine or the Opera.

'Place Clichy?'

'Yes.'

On the way, he did not say a word, and once they were at Place Clichy he simply muttered:

'Go up Rue Caulaincourt, not too fast, as if you're trying to read the house numbers.'

Near the boulevards, the streets were quite busy, and almost everywhere people were taking the air at their open windows. There were crowds, some of them rowdy, seated at the terraces of even the smallest cafés, and most of the restaurants were serving their customers outside.

It seemed impossible that a crime could be committed in those surroundings, and yet the conditions had been almost the same when Georgette Lecoin, the most recent victim, had been killed in Rue Tholozé, less than fifty metres from a dance hall with a red neon sign lighting up the pavement.

For anyone who really knew the area well, there were, not far from these animated main streets, a hundred deserted alleyways, a hundred dark corners where an attack could take place almost without risk.

Two minutes. They had calculated that the murderer had needed no more than two minutes and if he was quick even less.

What was it that drove him to lacerate his victim's clothes after committing murder?

He didn't touch the woman herself. There was no question here, as in certain other well known cases, of exposing the victim's private parts. He slashed the fabric with thrusts of a knife, as if in some kind of paroxysm of rage, like a child who savages a doll or stamps on a toy.

Tissot had talked about this too, but with reticence. One sensed that he was tempted to adopt some of the theories of Freud and his disciples, but it was as if he considered that too easy an explanation.

'We'd have to know about his past, including his childhood, and find the initial trauma, which he himself may have forgotten.'

Every time he thought like this about the murderer, Maigret was overcome with feverish impatience. He was in a hurry to imagine a face, precise features, a human silhouette, instead of the vague figure people were calling the killer, or the madman, or the monster, the figure whom Tissot, perhaps by an involuntary slip of the tongue, had called a 'patient'.

He was angered by his own powerlessness. It was almost as if he faced a personal challenge.

He would have liked to be able to confront the man, never mind where, look him full in the face and order him: 'Now, talk!'

He needed to know. The wait was agonizing, preventing him from giving his full attention to material details.

Automatically, yes, he was registering the positions of his men at the different points where he had posted them. He did not know them all. Many were not attached to his own division. But he still knew that a silhouette behind a certain window corresponded to a name, that a breathless woman hurrying past towards some unknown destination, taking short steps because of her high heels, was one of his auxiliary police officers. Since February and the first crime, the man had chosen a later hour every time to launch his attacks, from eight o'clock to nine forty-five. But what about now, when the days were getting shorter again instead of longer, and night was falling earlier?

At any moment, one might hear the cry of a passer-by

who had stumbled in the dark upon a body lying on the pavement. That was how most of the victims had been found, almost always after just a few minutes, and only once, according to the police pathologist, after about a quarter of an hour.

The car had gone past Rue Lamarck, and was entering an area where so far nothing had happened.

'What shall I do, sir?'

'Keep straight on, then come back via Rue des Abbesses.'

He could have remained in touch with some of his colleagues by using a radio car, but that would have been too conspicuous.

What was to say whether, before every attack, the man did not watch all comings and goings in the district for several hours?

Almost always, it is possible to sense when a murderer belongs to a particular category: even without a description, one has a general idea of what he might look like, what social background he comes from.

Please don't let there be another victim tonight!

This was a prayer, such as he used to offer up at bedtime, in his childhood. He did not even realize this.

'See that?'

'What?'

'The drunk under the streetlamp.'

'Who is it?'

'Friend of mine, Dutilleux. Loves dressing up. Especially as a drunk.'

At a quarter to ten, still nothing had happened.

'Stop by the Brasserie Pigalle.'

Maigret ordered a beer as he walked past the counter, then shut himself in the phone booth to call headquarters. It was Lucas who replied.

'Nothing?'

'Nothing yet. A streetwalker who's complaining she was harassed by a foreign sailor.'

'Torrence with you?'

'Yes.'

'And the Baron?'

'He must have gone home to bed.'

The time at which the last crime had been committed had gone past. Did that mean the man was less concerned with the darkness of the street than with the time of day? Or that the false arrest had had no effect on him?

Maigret had an ironic smile on his face as he returned to the car, and the irony was addressed to himself. Who knows? The man he was tracking through the streets of Montmartre might at this very moment be on holiday at some seaside resort in Normandy, or in a family hotel somewhere in the French countryside. A wave of despondency suddenly engulfed him, from one moment to the next. His efforts and those of all his colleagues appeared to him to be vain, bordering on ridiculous.

On what had he based this whole charade, which had taken so long to organize? On nothing. Less than nothing! On a sort of intuition he had had after a good dinner, while chatting in Pardon's peaceful drawing room with Professor Tissot.

But surely Tissot himself would have been alarmed, had he learned where their informal conversation had led?

And what if this man were *not* driven by pride, by the need to assert himself?

He could not now recall all those words he had pronounced, as if he were making a discovery, without feeling sick at heart. He had thought too much about it. He had worried away at the problem too long. He had lost belief in it now, almost doubting the reality of the killer.

'Where to, sir?'

'Wherever you like.'

The astonishment he saw in the eyes of the driver as he turned his head towards him made him aware of his own discouragement, and he felt ashamed. He had no right to lose faith in front of his own colleagues.

'Go up Rue Lepic, to the top.'

He passed the Moulin de la Galette nightclub, and looked at the exact spot on the pavement where they had found the body of Joséphine Simmer, the midwife.

So it *was* all real, here and now. Five crimes had been committed. And the killer was still at large, perhaps ready to strike again.

Was that hatless woman aged forty or so, scurrying down the street with a poodle on a lead, one of the police auxiliaries?

There were others in the nearby streets, risking their lives at this very instant. They were all volunteers. But it was Maigret who had given them their task. It was his responsibility to protect them.

Had all the necessary measures been taken?

That afternoon, on paper, the plan had looked faultless. Every area considered dangerous was being watched. The policewomen would be on their guard. Invisible watchers would be nearby, ready to intervene.

But had some corner been forgotten? Might someone not relax their attention for only a minute?

After the discouragement, he was starting to be overcome by a feeling of panic, which might have prompted him to cancel the whole operation, had it still been possible.

Perhaps the experiment had lasted long enough? It was ten o'clock. Nothing had happened. Nothing *would* happen now, and that was just as well.

On Place du Tertre, high up in Montmartre, there was a festive atmosphere, people were crowding round the little tables where rosé wine was being served and music could be heard from every corner; a fire-eater was performing and another man, despite the noise, was doggedly sawing away at a tune from 1900 on the violin. Yet a hundred metres further on, the little alleyways were deserted, and the killer might find it easy to pounce without risk.

'Go back down again.'

'Same way?'

He would have done better just to stick to the traditional approach, even if it was slow, even if it had produced no results in six months.

'Head for Place Constantin-Pecqueur.'

'Via Avenue Junot?'

'Yes, if you like.'

A few couples were walking arm in arm along the pavements, and Maigret spotted one couple locked in an embrace, their eyes closed, in a corner under a gas lamp.

Two cafés were still open on Place Constantin-Pecqueur, and there was no light showing in Lognon's apartment. The local inspector, who knew these streets better than anyone, was patrolling them on foot, like a gundog beating the bushes, and for a moment Maigret imagined him with his tongue hanging out, panting hot breaths like a spaniel.

'What time is it?'

'Ten past ten.'

'Hush!'

They strained their ears, and vaguely sensed the sound of people running towards Avenue Junot, the street they had just driven down.

And before the footsteps, there had been something else – possibly a blast on a whistle, or even two.

'Where's it coming from?'

'I don't know.'

It was hard to make out the exact direction from which the sounds had come. While the car was still stationary, a black vehicle from police headquarters hurtled past them, heading at top speed towards Avenue Junot.

'Follow that one!'

Other parked cars, only minutes earlier, had moved off as well, all heading in the same direction, and two more whistle-blasts came through the air, nearer now that Maigret's car had already driven five hundred metres.

They could hear voices, men and women. Someone was running along a pavement and another silhouette was dashing down the stone steps.

Something had happened at last.

4. *The Policewoman's Encounter*

Everything was so confused at first, in the poorly lit streets, that it was impossible to find out what had happened. Only much later, by putting together the witness statements, some more reliable than others, did an overall picture become clearer.

Maigret, whose driver was driving hell for leather through steep and narrow streets that at night looked like theatre sets, was not sure exactly where he was, except that they seemed to be approaching Place du Tertre, from where vague sounds of music reached his ears.

What added to the confusion was that things were moving in both directions. Cars, and running figures – most of them police officers, no doubt – were converging towards a point which seemed to be on Rue Norvins, while other silhouettes, a bicycle without lights, two, then three cars, were on the contrary moving quickly in the opposite direction.

'That way!' someone was shouting. 'I saw him go past!'

People were chasing a man, possibly one of those whom Maigret had seen. He also thought he had recognized, in a small figure running so fast that he had lost his hat, Inspector Hard-done-by but he couldn't be sure.

What mattered most to him at this moment was finding out whether the killer had been successful, whether a woman was dead, and when he saw a knot of about a dozen people standing on a shadowy pavement, his eyes turned anxiously to the ground at their feet.

The people did not seem to be looking downwards, though. He could see them gesticulating, and at the corner of an alleyway a uniformed policeman, sprung from somewhere, was trying to fend off curious onlookers flocking over from Place du Tertre.

Someone loomed out of the darkness and approached him as he climbed out of the car.

'Is that you, boss?'

The beam of an electric torch flashed over his face as if everyone distrusted everyone else.

'She's not injured.'

It took him a little time to identify the speaker, although he was an inspector from his own service.

'What happened?'

'I don't rightly know. The man managed to escape. They've gone after him. Be surprising if he gets away, with the whole district looking for him.'

At last, Maigret reached the centre of all the agitation, a woman in a light-blue dress that reminded him of something. Her bosom was still heaving rapidly. She was beginning to smile again, the fragile smile of someone who has just escaped death by inches.

She recognized Maigret.

'I'm sorry I didn't manage to grab him,' she said. 'I'm still wondering how he slipped out of my hands.'

She was uncertain now to whom she had already told the beginning of her story.

'Look! One of the buttons of his jacket came off in my hand.'

She held it out to the chief inspector: a small smooth, dark object, with a short length of thread and even a scrap of material still attached to it.

'He attacked you?'

'Just as I was going past this little alley.'

A narrow corridor, pitch dark, without a door opening on to the street.

'I was keeping my eyes open. When I saw the alleyway, I had a sort of intuition, and I had to make an effort to keep walking at the same pace.'

Now Maigret thought he recognized her, or at any rate the blue dress. Wasn't this the same girl he had seen a little while ago, under the streetlamp, locked in a close embrace with a man?

'He let me get past the opening, and just then, I sensed a movement, the air stirring behind me. A hand went for my throat, and I don't know how, but I managed to get a judo hold on him.'

News of what had happened must have spread to Place du Tertre, and most of the night owls had abandoned the tables with their red check cloths, the Chinese lanterns and the carafes of rosé wine, to come running in the same direction. The uniformed officer was overwhelmed. A police van was coming up Rue Caulaincourt. An attempt would be made to contain the crowds.

How many inspectors were now chasing after the fugitive through the neighbouring streets, a maze of unpredictable twists and turns with many dark corners?

Maigret had the feeling that in this respect at any rate, the game was already lost. Once more, the killer had demonstrated his genius by operating a mere hundred metres from a highly frequented tourist area, knowing full well that once the alert was sounded, the crowds would create chaos.

As far as he could recall – he did not take the time to consult his battle plan – Mauvoisin was in charge of this sector and would consequently be directing operations. He looked round for him, but he was not in sight.

Maigret's presence served no purpose here. From now on, it was a matter of luck.

'Get into my car,' he told the young woman.

He knew her to be one of his auxiliaries, and he was still somewhat ruffled at having seen her in a man's arms only a short while ago.

'What is your name?'

'Marthe Jusserand.'

'You're twenty-two?'

'Twenty-five.'

She was more or less of the same build as the five victims, but in her case the bulk came from muscle.

'Back to headquarters,' Maigret ordered the driver.

From his perspective, it would be best if he were at the point where all reports would inevitably converge, rather than hanging about here where the frantic activity seemed chaotic.

A little further on, he spotted Mauvoisin, who was giving instructions to his colleagues.

'I'm on my way back to Quai des Orfèvres,' he called out to him. 'Keep me posted.'

A radio car was arriving now. Two others, which were cruising in the locality, would be turning up soon, as reinforcements.

'Were you scared?' he asked his companion, as the car reached streets where the traffic was calmer. A crowd was spilling out of a cinema on Place Clichy. The bars and cafés were brightly lit and reassuring, with customers sitting out on the terraces.

'Not at the time, but straight afterwards. I thought my legs were going to give way.'

'Did you see him?'

'For a moment his face was very close to mine, but I'm not sure I'd be able to recognize him again. I spent three years as a gym teacher before I did my police exams, I'm quite strong, you know. I've done judo, like the other auxiliaries.'

'You didn't cry out?'

'I don't know.'

It was later ascertained, from an inspector who had been at a window in a nearby lodging house, that she had called for help only after the assailant had run off.

'He was wearing a darkish suit. His hair was light brown, he seemed quite young.'

'About how old, in your opinion?'

'I don't know. I was too shocked. I knew what I was supposed to do if he attacked, but when it happened, everything went out of my head. I was thinking about the knife he was holding.'

'You saw it?'

She was silent for a few seconds.

'I'm wondering now whether I really saw it, or whether

70

I just imagined it, because I knew he'd have one. On the other hand, I'd swear his eyes were blue or grey. He seemed to be in pain. I got a judo hold on his forearm, and it must have hurt him quite a bit. It was a matter of seconds before he was forced to bend over and fall on the ground.'

'And then he managed to break free.'

'Yes, I suppose he must have. He slipped through my fingers, and I still can't fathom how. I grabbed something, the button on his jacket, and next moment I just had the button in my hand and this shape was running away. It all happened very quickly. Though to me, of course, it seemed like a long time.'

'You wouldn't like a drink, would you, to help you get over it?'

'I never drink. But I wouldn't mind a cigarette.'

'Go ahead.'

'I haven't got any. A month ago, I decided to give up smoking.'

Maigret got the driver to stop at the next tobacconist's.

'What kind?'

'American.'

It must have been the first time in his life that he found himself buying American cigarettes.

At Quai des Orfèvres, he ushered her inside, and they found Lucas and Torrence each manning a telephone. Maigret looked inquiringly at them, and they both pulled negative faces.

The man hadn't been caught yet.

'Sit down, mademoiselle.'

'I'm feeling fine now . . . Never mind about the cigarette. It's in the next few days that it'll be hard not to smoke.'

Maigret repeated to Lucas, who had finished his phone call, the description he had been given.

'Send that out to everyone, including the railway stations.'

And to the young woman:

'How tall would you say?'

'No taller than me.'

So the man was quite short.

'Thin?'

'Not fat anyway.'

'Twenty? Thirty? Forty?'

She had said 'young' but the word can have quite different meanings.

'I'd say thirtyish.'

'No other detail you can remember?'

'No.'

'Was he wearing a tie?'

'I suppose so.'

'Did he look like a prowler, or like a labourer, or an office worker?'

She was doing her best to cooperate but her memories were fragmented.

'It seems to me that if I'd seen him in the street in any other circumstances, I wouldn't have noticed him. Respectable-looking, as they say.'

Suddenly she raised her hand, like a pupil in class – and after all it was not so long ago that she had been a school-girl.

'He had a ring on his finger!'

'A wedding ring, or some other kind?'

'Wait a minute . . .'

She closed her eyes, seemed to take again the pose she had been in during the struggle.

'I felt it under my fingers, then when I was doing the judo hold, his hand was near my face . . . Not a signet ring, that would have been too big with a bulge in it . . . It was certainly a wedding ring.'

'Hear that, Lucas?'

'Yes, boss.'

'His hair, long or short?'

'Not short. I can see his hair now, it was covering his ear when his head was almost on the pavement.'

'Still taking notes, Lucas?'

'Yes.'

'Come into my office, mademoiselle.'

He automatically removed his jacket, although by now the evening was quite cool, at least compared to daytime.

'Sit down. Are you sure you won't have something to drink?'

'Yes, sure.'

'Before the man attacked you, did you not meet somebody else?'

A rush of blood flooded up into her neck and cheeks. She was a muscular and athletic woman, but her skin was fair and delicate.

'Yes.'

'Tell me all about it.'

'Well, I may have done wrong, but I suppose that's too bad. I have a fiancé.'

73

'What does he do?'

'He's in his last year of law school. He wants to join the police too.'

Not the way Maigret had joined the force in the past, going up through the ranks, and starting in traffic control, but by passing a competitive graduate examination.

'And you saw him tonight?'

'Yes.'

'Did you tell him what this was all about?'

'No, I just asked him to spend the evening on Place du Tertre.'

'You were afraid?'

'No. I just wanted to feel he wasn't far away.'

'And you arranged to meet him again afterwards?'

She was ill at ease, shifting from one foot to another, trying to work out from brief glances whether Maigret was angry or not.

'I'll tell you the whole truth, sir. And too bad if I have made a mistake about this. My instructions were to act as naturally as possible, like any other girl or woman who might find herself walking along a street this evening. Well, at night, you often see couples who kiss goodbye and then go their separate ways.'

'Was that why you had your fiancé come along?'

'Yes, I promise you. I arranged to meet him at ten. We were assuming that if anything happened, it would be before ten. So I wasn't risking anything if at ten o'clock I thought of trying another tactic.'

Maigret looked attentively at her.

'It didn't occur to you that if the murderer saw you in

the arms of another man and then going off down the road alone, that that might trigger his crisis?'

'I don't know. I suppose there was a chance. Did I do wrong?'

He preferred not to reply. It was always a dilemma, to choose between observing discipline and showing initiative. Had he not himself, tonight and on the preceding days, committed some serious infringements to discipline?

'Take your time. Sit down at my desk. What you're going to do is, as if you were in school, write down what happened this evening, trying to remember the tiniest details, even ones that don't seem at all important.'

He knew from experience that this often yields results.

'May I use your pen?'

'If you like. Call me when you've finished.'

He went back into the office where Lucas and Torrence were still sharing the phone calls. In a box room at the end of the corridor, a radio-telegraphist was noting the messages received from the radio cars, which he then dispatched on scraps of paper via the office clerk.

Up in Montmartre, they had gradually managed to disperse most of the crowds, but as was to be expected, reporters alerted by the news had come flocking to the site.

The police had at first surrounded three blocks of houses, then four, then the whole district, as time passed and the man had had more opportunities to make his getaway.

The local hotels and lodging houses had been visited, all lodgers and guests being woken up, asked for their papers, and obliged to answer a few questions. There was every chance that the attacker had already slipped through the net, probably in the first few minutes, just when the whistle was heard, when people started to run and Place du Tertre had spilled out its flock of sightseers.

There was another possibility: that the killer lived nearby, not far from the site of this latest attack, and that he had simply gone home.

Maigret toyed with the button that Marthe Jusserand had left with him, an ordinary button, dark grey with light blue streaks. No maker's name. Some stout tailor's thread was still attached to it, as well as a fragment of fabric, a few strands of a tweed suit.

'Telephone Moers and get him to come over at once.'

'Here, or to the lab?'

'Here.'

He had learned from experience that an hour lost at a critical point in an investigation could represent a head start of several weeks for the criminal.

'Lognon wants to speak to you, sir.'

'Where is he?'

'In some café in Montmartre.'

'Hello! Lognon?'

'Yes, boss. They're still hunting for him. They've closed off a big chunk of the district. But I'm pretty sure he's the man I saw running down the steps, just opposite where I live, Place Constantin-Pecqueur.'

'And you couldn't catch up with him?'

'No, I ran as fast as I could, but he's much faster.'

'And you didn't shoot?'

Those had nevertheless been the orders: shoot on sight,

aiming for the legs if possible, on condition passers-by were not put at risk.

'I didn't dare because there was an old beggar-woman asleep on the bottom step, and I might have hit her. Then it was too late. He disappeared into the shadows, as if he'd faded into a wall. After that I searched the area, square metre by square metre, and all the time I had the feeling he wasn't far away, that he was watching my movements.'

'That's all?'

'Yes. My colleagues arrived and we did a collective search.'

'With no result?'

'Just this: a man apparently went in at about that time to a bar in Rue Caulaincourt, where customers were playing belote. Without stopping at the counter, he went into the phone booth, which means he must have had telephone tokens. He made a call, then he went out again as he had come in, not a word or a glance to the barman or the drinkers. That's why they noticed. The people in that bar had no idea what was going on.'

'Anything else?'

'This man is described as fair-haired, youngish, thin, no hat.'

'His suit?'

'Dark coloured. My thoughts are that he called someone who came to pick him up in a car at a prearranged spot. We didn't think of stopping cars with more than one occupant.'

It would be the first time in the annals of crime, indeed, that a maniac of this kind was not operating on his own.

'Thanks anyway, my friend.'

'I'll stay on the spot. We'll keep looking.'

'It's all we can do.'

It might just have been a coincidence. After all, anyone can go into a café simply to use the telephone, without having time to stop for a drink. But it troubled Maigret all the same. He wondered about the wedding ring the police-woman had remembered.

Could it be that in order to escape from the police cordon, the man had had the gall to telephone his wife? In that case, what excuse would he have given her? In tomorrow's newspapers, she would surely read about what had happened in Montmartre.

'Is Moers here yet?'

'He'll be along any moment. He was reading in bed. I told him to get a taxi.'

Marthe Jusserand brought him her essay, that is, her report on the events as she had experienced them.

'I didn't try to write it up in a fancy way, just to put it all down as objectively as possible.'

He ran his eye over the two sheets of paper without noting anything new, and it was only when the young woman turned round to pick up her handbag that he noticed that her dress was slashed at the back. That detail suddenly made concrete the danger Maigret had placed her in, along with the other women auxiliaries.

'You can go home to bed now. I'll get someone to drive you.'

'There's no need, sir. Jean will certainly be downstairs with his car.'

He looked at her with an amused expression.

'But you couldn't have asked him to meet you here at headquarters, could you, since you didn't know you would end up here.'

'No. But he was one of the first people to arrive from Place du Tertre. I spotted him among all the people staring and the inspectors. He saw me talking to you and getting into your car. He will be sure to have guessed you were bringing me here.'

Astonished, Maigret could only murmur as he shook hands with her:

'Well, my dear, I wish you all the luck in the world with your Jean. Thank you. And I apologize for all the turmoil I have put you through. Of course, the press must not learn a whisper about the trap we laid. We will not be letting them know your name.'

'Good, I'd prefer it that way.'

'Goodnight.'

He accompanied her courteously to the top of the stairs and returned to his inspectors, shaking his head.

'Strange girl,' he grunted.

Torrence, who had his own ideas about the younger generation, commented quietly:

'The girls are all like that, these days.'

Moers entered the room a few minutes later, looking as fresh as if he had had a good night's sleep. He knew nothing of the evening's events. The plans to entrap the killer had not been communicated to the laboratory staff.

'Some work for me, boss?'

Maigret held out the button and Moers pulled a face.

'That's all?'

'Yes.'

Moers turned it over several times in his hand.

'Want me to go upstairs and examine it?'

'I'll come with you.'

It was almost out of superstition. The telephone calls kept coming in, one after another. Maigret still did not feel confident. Yet every time the phone rang, he could hardly help giving a start, hoping that the miracle had happened. Perhaps if he wasn't on the spot it would transpire after all, and they would come to the laboratory and tell him that the killer had been caught.

Moers switched on the lights, and picked up first a magnifying glass, then tweezers, and a whole series of delicate instruments, before he examined the thread and the scraps of fabric under the microscope.

'I suppose you'd like to know where the garment was made that this button came from?'

'I want to know everything there is to know about it.'

'Well, first the button, although it looks quite ordinary, is actually of very good quality. It's not the kind used for mass-produced clothes. I think it shouldn't be too difficult tomorrow morning to find out where it was made, because there aren't many button manufacturers. They nearly all have offices in Rue des Petits-Champs, close to the wholesale drapers.'

'And the thread?'

'It's the kind most tailors use. The cloth is more interesting. As you can see, the weave is an ordinary grey but there's a light-blue strand which makes it typical of its kind. I'd be prepared to bet this isn't French-made suiting, but tweed imported from England. There are relatively few firms that handle such imports, and I can give you the list.'

Moers possessed lists of all kinds, directories, catalogues, which he used to determine very quickly the origin of an object, whether a gun, a pair of shoes or a pocket handkerchief.

'And look! As you can see, most of the importers also have offices in Rue des Petits-Champs.'

Luckily, the wholesalers still had their headquarters more or less grouped in certain districts of Paris.

'None of these offices will be open until eight in the morning, most of them only at nine.'

'I'll have the men make a start with the ones that open at eight.'

'Is that all for tonight?'

'Unless you think of anything else we should be doing.'

'I'll try, just in case.'

He would no doubt be scrutinizing the thread and the scraps of tweed for some dust or other incriminating substance. After all, three years earlier, had they not identified one criminal thanks to traces of sawdust on a handkerchief, and another through a spot of printer's ink?

Maigret suddenly felt tired. The tension of the last days and hours had dropped and he found himself without energy, without a wish for anything, without optimism.

Tomorrow morning, he would have to face Coméliau, and the journalists who would besiege him with awkward questions. What was he going to tell them? He couldn't tell them the truth. But neither did he want to embark on a pack of lies.

When he went back down to the Police Judiciaire, he realized that the ordeal by the press would not be for tomorrow, but straightaway. Although the Baron wasn't there, three other reporters were, including young Rougin, whose eyes were bright with excitement.

'May we have a word in your office, chief inspector?'

Shrugging his shoulders, Maigret let them in and looked at the three of them standing there, notepads in hand and pencils at the ready.

'So did your prisoner escape?'

Inevitably they would start there, with the man whose existence had become an embarrassment, now that events had taken a sudden new course.

'No one has escaped.'

'Did you release him then?'

'No one has been released.'

'But tonight there was another attempted murder, wasn't there?'

'A young woman was indeed attacked in the street, not far from Place du Tertre, but she got away with just a fright.'

'She wasn't injured?'

'No.'

'Did her attacker have a knife?'

'She's not sure about that.'

'She isn't here now?'

They were peering round suspiciously. No doubt they had been told up in Montmartre that the young woman had been seen getting into Maigret's car.

'What's her name?'

'Her name's not important.'

'Are you keeping it a secret?'

'Let's just say that it would serve no purpose to publish it.'

'Why not? Is she married? Was she somewhere she shouldn't have been?'

'That might be one reason.'

'The right one?'

'I wouldn't know.'

'Don't you think this is all becoming very mysterious?'

'The only mystery that concerns me is the identity of the killer.'

'And have you discovered that?'

'Not yet.'

'Have you got any new elements that might help you discover it?'

'Possibly.'

'But of course you're not going to tell us about them?'

'No, of course not.'

'Did this young lady with the secret name see her assailant?'

'Not clearly, but enough for me to be able to give you a description.'

Maigret told them the few details she had recalled, but without mentioning the button torn from the jacket.

'That's pretty vague, isn't it?'

'Yesterday things were vaguer still, since we knew nothing at all about him.'

He was in a bad mood, irritated with himself for having to treat them this way. They were simply doing their job, as he was. He knew he was infuriating them by his answers, and even more by his silences, but he could not make himself act in his usual cordial manner.

'I'm very tired, gentlemen.'

'Are you going home?'

'As soon as you let me get away.'

'Are they still looking for him up there?'

'Yes.'

'Are you going to release the man Inspector Lognon brought up here the day before yesterday, the one you interrogated twice?'

He had to provide them with an answer to this question.

'That man was not being interrogated. He wasn't a suspect but a witness whose identity could not, for certain reasons, be divulged.'

'As a precaution?'

'Perhaps.'

'Is he still under police guard?'

'Yes.'

'And there was no possibility he could have been in Montmartre this evening?'

'No. Any more questions?'

'When we got here, you were up in the laboratory.'

They knew the layout of the building as well as he did.

'Up there, they don't work on hunches but on evidence.'

He stared at them without flinching.

'May we conclude that the man in Rue Norvins left something behind, perhaps in the victim's hands?'

'It would be better, in the interests of the investigation, if you were not to draw any conclusions from my comings and goings. Gentlemen, I am quite exhausted, and I would ask you to let me go home now. In twenty-four or perhaps forty-eight hours, I may have something to tell you. Meanwhile, you will have to be satisfied with the description of the attacker I have given you.'

It was half past one in the morning. In the next office, the telephone calls were coming in less frequently, and he went to bid goodnight to Torrence and Lucas.

'Still nothing?'

He had only to look at them to see that the question was pointless. The police would still be scouring the Montmartre area, street by street, house by house, until the dawn lit up the dustbins pulled out on to the edge of the pavements.

'Goodnight, boys.'

He had kept on the car, in case of further need, and the driver was pacing round the courtyard. To find a place open for a glass of cool beer, he would have had to go as far as Montparnasse or the other way, up to Pigalle, and he had no heart for that.

Madame Maigret, in her nightdress, opened the door before he had time to get his key out of his pocket, and he headed gloomily and with an obstinate frown towards the sideboard where the bottle of plum brandy was kept. He really wanted a beer, not a liqueur, but as he drank off his glass in a single gulp, he had a slight feeling he was getting his revenge.

5. *The Cigarette Burn*

It could have taken weeks. Everyone at Quai des Orfèvres that morning was worn out, with a bad taste in the mouth. Some people, Maigret among them, had slept for three or four hours. Others, who lived out in the suburbs, had not slept at all.

A search of the Grandes-Carrières neighbourhood was still going on, with police watching the Métro stations, and observing any men coming out of buildings.

'Sleep well, chief inspector?'

It was young Rougin, as fresh as a daisy, and more ebullient than usual, calling out from the corridor, in his high-pitched, rather strident voice. He seemed in particularly good humour this morning, and Maigret discovered why only when he picked up the newspaper to which the young reporter was attached. Rougin too had taken a risk. Already, the previous day, then again during the evening, and finally when three or four of them had arrived to pester him, Rougin had suspected the truth.

He had probably spent the rest of the night asking questions of certain people, hotel proprietors in particular.

At any rate, his newspaper carried a banner headline:

Killer escapes police trap!

In the corridor, Rougin must have been waiting to see Maigret's reaction.

> *Our good friend, Detective Chief Inspector Maigret* [his article ran] *will probably not dissent if we say that the arrest carried out two days ago, and surrounded deliberately with much mystery, was a trick, intended to draw the Montmartre killer into a trap.*

Rougin had gone even further. He had woken a renowned psychiatrist in the middle of the night, and asked him questions very like those Maigret had put to Professor Tissot.

> *Were they calculating that the murderer would come and prowl round police headquarters, to catch a glimpse of the man they had arrested instead of him? That is one possibility. But it is more likely that they hoped, by wounding his vanity, to provoke him into another attack, in a district which had been well staked out with police officers beforehand.*

It was the only newspaper to have taken this line. The other reporters were all in the dark.

'Still here?' grunted Maigret, when he saw Lucas. 'Don't you have a home to go to?'

'I slept in an armchair, then I went for a dip in the Deligny Baths and I shaved in my cabin.'

'Who's available?'

'Almost everyone.'

'And nothing to report, naturally . . .'

Lucas merely shrugged his shoulders.

'Get Janvier and Lapointe and two or three others.'

All he had drunk the previous night was a beer and a glass of plum brandy, but he still felt a bitter aftertaste. The sky was overcast but not with real clouds, which might have brought cooler air. A greyish veil had gradually gathered over the city, a sticky kind of haze slowly covering the streets, laden with dust and petrol fumes that caught in the throat.

Maigret opened his window but shut it again at once, since the air outside was even more unbreathable than in his office.

'Now, then, you're going to go straight over to Rue des Petits-Champs. Here are a few addresses. If you have no luck with these, try others that you can find from the street directory. Some of them handle buttons, others suiting.'

He explained what Moers had told him about the wholesalers and importers:

'We just might be lucky this time. Keep me posted.'

He was still in the same bad mood, and it was not, as everyone believed, because his plan had failed, because the man they were searching for had slipped through the net.

He had expected that. The plan had not, in fact, been a failure, since his prediction had been confirmed and now at last they had a clue, something to work with, however insignificant it seemed.

His mind was focusing on the killer, who was beginning to take shape in his mind, since at least one person had caught sight of him. He envisaged him as a youngish man, with light-coloured hair, probably melancholy or bitter.

Why would Maigret have laid money just now that he came from a good family, and was accustomed to a comfortable way of life?

He wore a wedding ring. So he had a wife. He had had a father and mother. He had been a schoolboy, perhaps a university student.

And this morning he was alone, against the Paris police force, against the entire Parisian population, and he would also, no doubt, have read Rougin's article in the paper.

Had he slept, once he had escaped the dragnet which had almost caught him?

If his crimes brought him a kind of release, euphoria even, what effect would a failed attempt produce?

Maigret did not wait for Coméliau to call him in, but went straight to his office, where he found the magistrate reading the papers.

'I did warn you, Maigret. You can't argue either that I showed any enthusiasm for your plan, or that I approved of it.'

'My men are following up a lead.'

'A serious one?'

'They are in possession of a material clue. It will inevitably lead us somewhere. It might take weeks, or it could take a couple of hours.'

In the event, it was less than two hours.

Lapointe, on reaching Rue des Petits-Champs, had first gone to a set of offices where the walls were covered with buttons of every shape and size. *Purveyors of buttons since 1782* read a sign over the door, with the names of the two partners. And the collection on the walls was an exhibition of all the models of button manufactured since the company had been founded.

After showing his police badge, Lapointe had asked:

'Would it be possible to tell where this button comes from?'

For him, for Maigret and for the man in the street, it was just a button like any other, but the clerk who examined it replied without hesitation:

'It comes from Mullerbach's in Colmar.'

'Does Mullerbach have a Paris office?'

'Yes, in this building, two floors up.'

In fact, the entire building, as Lapointe and his colleague now realized, was occupied by button manufacturers.

There was no Monsieur Mullerbach these days; but the son of the last Monsieur Mullerbach's son-in-law was in charge. He received the two policemen courteously in his office, and turned the button over in his hands.

'What is it exactly that you want to know?'

'Did your firm make this button?'

'Yes.'

'Do you have a list of the tailors to whom you would have sold ones like this?'

The industrialist pressed a bell and explained:

'As you may know, the wholesale drapers change the colours and sometimes the weave of their fabrics every year. Before they put the new types on sale, they send up samples, so that we can make buttons to match. And those are sold directly to the tailors.'

A young man who seemed to be wilting in the heat entered the room.

'Monsieur Jeanfils, would you kindly find the reference number for this button and bring me the list of the tailors to whom we have sold ones like it?'

Jeanfils went out without having opened his mouth. In his absence, his employer went on to explain to the policemen how sales of buttons were organized. Less than ten minutes later, there was a knock on the glass panel of the door. The same Jeanfils came in and placed the button on the desk with a typewritten sheet of paper.

It was a list of about forty tailors: four in Lyon, two in Bordeaux, one in Lille, a few others in various French cities and the rest in Paris.

'Here you are, gentlemen. I wish you luck.'

They found themselves back in the street, its hubbub almost shocking after the offices, which had been as calm and quiet as a church sacristy.

'What should we do?' asked Broncard, who was working with Lapointe. 'Start right away? I counted. There are twenty-eight in Paris. If we took a taxi . . .'

'Do you know where Janvier went?'

'Yes, into that big building over there, or rather into the offices through the courtyard.'

'Wait here for him.'

Lapointe went into a little bar with sawdust on the floor, ordered a white wine and Vichy water and shut himself in the phone booth. Maigret was still with Coméliau, so the operator put him straight through to the magistrate's office.

'Forty tailors in all,' he explained. 'Twenty-eight of them in Paris. Shall I make a start?'

'Just take four or five names yourself, and dictate the rest to Lucas, he can send some men round.'

He had hardly finished dictating the list when Janvier, Broncard and a fourth policeman entered the bar and waited for him at the counter. They were all three looking pleased with themselves. After a moment, Janvier opened the door of the booth.

'Don't hang up, I need to speak to him.'

'It's not the boss on the line now, it's Lucas.'

'Pass him on to me, even so.'

For lack of sleep, they were all slightly feverish and their breath was hot, their eyes bright with fatigue.

'That you, Lucas? Tell the boss it's going well. Yes. Janvier here. We've hit the bull's eye! It was really a stroke of luck, the man was wearing a suit made of English tweed. I'll explain. I know how it works now. There are only about a dozen tailors up to now who've ordered this material. Many more received sample swatches. What they do is, they show the samples to the customer, and then if he orders a suit, they get hold of an appropriate length. So we're hopeful we can be on to this quickly, unless the suit was made in England, which is pretty unlikely.'

They split up outside the bar, each with two or three names on a piece of paper, and it was as if they were running a lottery between them. One of the four men would, in all likelihood, and perhaps this very morning, find out the name they had been after for six months.

It was Lapointe who had drawn the winning ticket. He had taken the Left Bank, the area round Boulevard Saint-Germain, which he knew well because he lived there.

The first tailor he visited, on Boulevard Saint-Michel, had indeed ordered a length of this precious suiting fabric. He was even able to show the inspector the suit he had made from it, since it hadn't yet been delivered to the customer, and in fact was not quite finished. With one sleeve and the collar to complete, he was waiting for the customer to come for a fitting.

The second was a little Polish tailor up on a third floor in Rue Vanneau. He had only one assistant. Lapointe found him sitting cross-legged on his table, wearing steel-rimmed spectacles.

'Do you recognize this material?'

Janvier had requested several samples from the wholesaler to share with his colleagues.

'Yes, why? Would you like a suit made in it?'

'I want the name of the customer for whom you made one.'

'It was a while back.'

'How long?'

'Last autumn.'

'You don't remember the customer's name?'

'Yes, I do.'

'Who was it?'

'Monsieur Moncin, Marcel.'

'And who's Monsieur Moncin?'

'Well, he's a very respectable gentleman, I've been making his suits for a few years now.'

Lapointe was trembling, hardly able to believe it. The miracle was happening. The man they had been hunting so long, about whom so much printer's ink had been spilled, to whom so many hours of police time had been devoted, suddenly had a name. He was going to have an address, a civil identity, and before long, no doubt, he would have taken physical shape.

'Does he live nearby?'

'Not far from here, Boulevard Saint-Germain, near Solférino Métro station.'

'You know him well, do you?'

'Like all my customers. He's very polite, a charming man.'

'Has he been to see you recently?'

'Last time was in November, about an overcoat, not long after I made the suit for him.'

'Do you have his exact address?'

The little tailor looked through a notebook where names and addresses were pencilled in, alongside numbers indicating the prices of clothes no doubt, which he ticked off in red when they had been paid for.

'228a.'

'Do you know whether he's married?'

'His wife's been in with him several times. She always comes when he has to make up his mind about something.'

'Is she young?'

'About thirty, I should think. She's very distinguished, a real lady.'

Lapointe could not control the trembling which had now taken over his entire body. It was verging on panic. So close to the goal, he was afraid there would be some sudden hitch that would send everything into doubt again.

'Thank you. I may be back to see you again.'

He had forgotten to ask what Marcel Moncin's profession was, as he rushed down the stairs and hurried along Boulevard Saint-Germain, where the building with the number 228a now appeared fascinating to him. And yet it was just a nineteenth-century apartment building, in the same style as all the neighbouring blocks on the boulevard, with wrought-iron balconies. The street door stood open on to a beige-painted corridor, at the end of which a lift was visible. The concierge's lodge was on the right.

He felt an almost painful desire to go inside, to ask the concierge for information, then go up to Moncin's apartment, to finish with the famous killer once and for all, on his own. But he knew he had no right to do such a thing.

Just opposite the Métro entrance, a uniformed policeman was on duty, and Lapointe went over and identified himself.

'Can you keep an eye on that building for a few minutes? I need to call headquarters.'

'What do you want me to do?'

'Nothing. Or no, rather, if a man aged about thirty, slim, fairish hair, happens to come out, can you find some excuse to hold on to him, ask him for his identity papers, anything you can think of.'

'Who is he?'

'His name's Marcel Moncin.'

'What's he done?'

Lapointe preferred not to make it clear that most probably he was the Montmartre murderer. A few moments later, he was in another café, telephoning.

'Is that Quai des Orfèvres? Get me Detective Chief Inspector Maigret right away. Lapointe speaking.'

He was so feverish that he was stuttering.

'Boss, is that you? La-Lapointe here. Yes. Found him . . . How? . . . Yes . . . Name and address. I'm standing right opposite where he lives.'

He was suddenly struck by the idea that other suits had been made from the same fabric, and that perhaps his man wasn't the right one.

'Janvier hasn't phoned, has he? Yes? What did he say?'

They had tracked down three other suits, but none of the men corresponded at all to the description given by Marthe Jusserand.

'I'm phoning from Boulevard Saint-Germain. I've got an officer watching the door. Yes, yes . . . I'll wait for you . . . Just a minute, I'll check the name of this café.'

He came out of the booth, and read backwards the name enamelled on the outside window.

'Café Solférino.'

Maigret had told him to stay there without showing himself. Less than a quarter of an hour later, as he stood at the counter in front of another white wine and Vichy water, he recognized a number of small police cars parking at different places.

From one of them, Maigret in person got out, and to Lapointe he looked more massive and heavily built than ever.

'It was so easy, boss, that I hardly dare believe it.'

Was Maigret as nervous as he was himself?

If so, it didn't show. Or rather, for those who knew him

well, it betrayed itself in his grumpy and dogged demeanour.

'What are you drinking?'

'A white wine and Vichy water.'

Maigret pulled a face.

'Do you have draught beer here?'

'Of course, Monsieur Maigret!'

'You know me?'

'I've seen your picture in the papers plenty of times. And last year, when you were investigating something in the ministry offices across the road, you came in for a drink now and then.'

He drank up his beer.

'Come along.'

During that time, a number of precautions had been taken, on a lesser scale than the night before, but no less effective. Two inspectors had gone up to the top floor of the building. Others were on the pavement outside the house, others still on the opposite side of the road and at the corner, and a radio car was nearby.

There was probably no need. Killers of this kind rarely put up any defence, certainly not an armed one.

'Shall I come with you?'

Maigret nodded and they both went towards the concierge's lodge. It was a comfortable, respectable-looking one, with a small sitting room divided from the kitchen by a red velvet curtain. The concierge, a woman of about fifty, was calm and smiling.

'Who did you want, gentlemen?'

'Monsieur Moncin, please?'

'Second floor left.'

'You don't know whether he's at home, do you?'

'He's probably there, because I haven't seen him go out.'

'Is Madame Moncin there as well?'

'She came back from shopping about half an hour ago.'

Maigret couldn't help thinking of his conversation with Professor Tissot at the Pardons'. This building was quiet and comfortable, and its old-fashioned atmosphere, its style dating from the previous century, had something reassuring about it. The lift, well maintained, with gleaming brass fittings, was waiting for them, but they preferred to go up on foot, treading on the thick crimson stair carpet.

Most of the doormats in front of the dark wooden doors bore initials picked out in red, and all the bell-pushes were polished; there was no sound to be heard from inside the apartments, and no smell of cooking in the stairwell.

One of the doors on the first floor carried a brass plate indicating that the occupant was a specialist in chest diseases.

On the second floor left, a similar brass plate carried the inscription in more stylish modern script:

Marcel Moncin
Architect-Interior Decorator

The two men stopped and looked at each other, and Lapointe had the sense that Maigret was as keyed up as himself. It was the chief inspector who reached out to press the bell. They couldn't hear it ring, so it must have sounded deep inside the apartment. A time that seemed rather long elapsed before finally the door opened, and a maidservant in a white apron, who could not be as much as twenty years old, stared at them in amazement and asked:

'What is it?'

'Is Monsieur Moncin at home?'

She seemed embarrassed and stammered:

'I . . . I don't know . . .'

So he was there.

'If you wait a moment, I'll go and ask madame.'

She had no need to go far. A woman who was still young appeared at the end of the corridor. On returning from shopping, she must have changed into a light peignoir because of the heat.

'What is it, Odile?'

'Two gentlemen who want to see monsieur, madame.'

She came forward, pulling the sides of the peignoir together and looking Maigret in the eye, as if he reminded her of someone.

'And you wanted . . . ?' she asked, trying to understand.

'Is your husband at home?'

'Well . . .'

'That means he is.'

She blushed slightly.

'Yes. But he's asleep.'

'I'm afraid I must ask you to wake him.'

She hesitated, then said quietly:

'To whom do I have the honour . . .'

'Police Judiciaire.'

'It's Chief Inspector Maigret, isn't it? I thought I recognized you . . .'

Maigret had unobtrusively moved forwards, and was now standing in the entrance hall.

'Would you wake your husband, please? I suppose he must have got in late last night?'

'What do you mean?'

'Does he usually sleep until eleven in the morning?'

She smiled.

'Quite often. He likes to work in the evenings, and it can go on late into the night. He's a creative person, an artist.'

'So he wasn't out last night?'

'Not as far as I know. If you would wait a little while in the drawing room, I'll go and get him up.'

She had opened the glass door into a drawing room which was furnished in a modern style, rather unexpected in this older building, but not aggressively so. Maigret thought that he could quite well live with a decor like this. Only the paintings on the walls, of which he made nothing at all, were displeasing.

Lapointe stayed on his feet and kept his eyes on the main door of the apartment. Not that he needed to, since by now all the exits were guarded. The young woman, who had departed with a swish of silk, was away only a few minutes and returned – not without having combed her hair.

'He'll be here in a moment. Marcel is rather shy and I tease him about it, but he doesn't like to meet people without being properly dressed.'

'You have separate bedrooms?'

She looked a little shocked at this, but replied simply:

'Like many married couples, surely.'

It was after all almost standard, in a certain social milieu. It didn't necessarily mean anything. What he was trying to discover was whether she was play-acting, whether she knew anything, or whether on the contrary she was genuinely wondering what possible connection there could be between Chief Inspector Maigret and her husband.

'Your husband works at home?'

'Yes.'

She went to open a side door which gave on to a quite spacious office, its two windows looking down on Boulevard Saint-Germain. Inside they glimpsed drawing boards, rolls of paper, and some curious models made of plaster and wire, reminiscent of stage sets.

'He works hard, does he?'

'Too hard for his health. He's never been strong. We should be away in the mountains, like other years, but he took on a commission that will prevent us from taking a holiday.'

He had rarely encountered a woman so calm and in control of herself. Shouldn't she be deeply alarmed – when the papers were full of stories about the murderer, and everyone knew Maigret was leading the investigation – to have him turn up on her doorstep? She was merely looking at him as if she were simply curious to meet such a famous man close up.

'I'll go and see if he's nearly ready.'

Maigret, sitting in an armchair, slowly filled his pipe, then lit it and exchanged a further glance with Lapointe, who could hardly keep still.

When the door through which Madame Moncin had

vanished opened again, they saw not her but a man who looked so young as to suggest their visit was a complete misunderstanding.

He was wearing indoor casual clothes of a light beige colour, which showed off his fair hair, delicate fine skin and pale blue eyes.

'My apologies, gentlemen, for keeping you waiting.'

A smile, in which there was something fragile and child-like, floated on his lips.

'My wife has just woken me up. She says . . .'

Was she not at all curious to find out the purpose of their visit? She had not come back. Perhaps she was listening outside the door, which her husband had now closed.

'I've been doing a lot of work lately, decorating a huge villa that a friend of mine is building on the Normandy coast.'

Pulling a fine lawn handkerchief from his pocket, he mopped his brow and patted his top lip, where beads of sweat had appeared.

'Even warmer than yesterday, isn't it?'

He looked outside at the lavender-coloured sky.

'It doesn't help to open the windows. I hope there's a storm on the way.'

'I must apologize,' Maigret began, 'but I have to ask you a few indiscreet questions. The first thing is that I would like to see the suit you were wearing yesterday.'

The question appeared to surprise him, but not to unnerve him. His eyes opened a little wider, and his lips pouted: his expression seemed to indicate:

'What an odd request!'

Then, as he went to the door:

'Excuse me for a moment.'

He was away only half a minute at most, and returned with a grey, well-pressed suit over his arm. Maigret examined it and found inside a pocket a label with the name of the little tailor in Rue Vanneau.

'This is what you were wearing yesterday?'

'Certainly.'

'And last night as well?'

'Until dinner. Then I changed into these more comfortable clothes before starting work. I tend to work all night.'

'And you didn't leave the house after eight?'

'I was in my office until two in the morning, or half past, which is why I was asleep when you arrived. I need a lot of sleep, like all people of a sensitive nature.'

He seemed to be asking for their approval, reminding them more of a student than of someone over thirty.

From close up, however, it was possible to see that his face was more gaunt than it had seemed, contradicting the impression of youth he had given at first. There was something tired and fragile about his complexion, not lacking in charm, as may happen with women of a certain age.

'May I ask you to show me your entire wardrobe?'

This time, he stiffened a little, and was perhaps on the point of protesting or refusing.

'If that is what you wish. This way.'

If his wife was waiting behind the door, she had had time to move away, since they could see her at the end of the corridor, talking to the maid in the light modern kitchen.

Moncin pushed open another door, to a bedroom with coffee-coloured walls, in the middle of which was an unmade divan-bed. He went to draw the curtains aside, as the room was dark, and opened the sliding doors of a fitted cupboard occupying the whole of one wall.

There were six lounge suits hanging up on the right, all immaculately pressed as if they had not been worn, or were just back from the dry-cleaners, and three overcoats, one lighter than the others, plus a dinner-jacket and a morning coat.

None of the suits matched the fabric in Lapointe's pocket.

'Can you pass me that material?' Maigret asked him.

He held it out to their host.

'Last autumn, your tailor delivered to you a suit made of this fabric. Do you remember?'

Moncin looked at the sample.

'Yes, I remember.'

'What has become of this suit now?'

He seemed to think.

'I know,' he said finally. 'I was on a bus and someone's cigarette scorched it.'

'And you sent it to be repaired?'

'No, I hate any object that's less than perfect. It's obsessive, I know, but I've been like this since I was a child. I used to throw away a toy if it was scratched.'

'So you threw away this suit? You mean you put it in the dustbin?'

'No, I gave it away.'

'Personally?'

'Yes. I picked it up one night when I was going out for a walk along the embankment, as I sometimes do, and I gave it to a tramp.'

'A long time ago?'

'Two or three days.'

'Can you be a bit more precise?'

'The day before yesterday.'

On the left-hand side of the cupboard, there were at least a dozen pairs of shoes lined up on shelves, and above them drawers containing shirts, underpants, pyjamas and handkerchiefs, all in impeccable order.

'Where are the shoes you were wearing last night?'

There was no intake of breath, and he did not appear troubled.

'I wasn't wearing shoes, just slippers, which I always wear in my office.'

'Would you call the maid? We can go back to the drawing room.'

'Odile,' he called in the direction of the kitchen. 'Come here for a minute.'

The maid gave the impression of having arrived only recently from the French countryside, of which she still had something of the bloom.

'Yes, monsieur.'

She did not seem troubled either, only a little excited to be in the presence of an official personality whose name was in the papers.

'Do you sleep overnight in the apartment?'

'No, monsieur, I have a room up on the sixth floor with the other maids in the building.'

'And did you go up there late last night?'

'At about nine o'clock, like I do nearly every day, after washing the dishes.'

'And where was Monsieur Moncin then?'

'In his office.'

'And can you tell me what he was wearing?'

'Same as he is now.'

'Sure about that, are you?'

'Yes, monsieur, certain.'

'Have you seen his grey suit lately, the one with a little blue thread in the pattern?'

She thought for a moment.

'I should say, sir, that I don't have much to do with monsieur's clothes. He's . . . very, er, particular about them.'

She had been on the point of saying something like 'fussy'.

'You mean he presses them himself?'

'Yes, that's right.'

'And you don't have permission to open his cupboards?'

'Only to put linen in, when it comes back from the laundry.'

'So you don't know when he last wore his grey suit with the blue thread?'

'I think it was two or three days ago.'

'You didn't by any chance, while you were serving at table, hear mention of the jacket being scorched by a cigarette?'

She looked at her employer as if to ask for his advice, and stammered:

'N-no, I, I don't think so. I don't listen to what monsieur

and madame talk about at table. They're usually talking about things I don't understand.'

'That's all, you may go.'

Marcel Moncin was waiting calmly, a smile on his face and just a few beads of sweat on his upper lip.

'I must ask you to dress for going out, if you will, and come with me to Quai des Orfèvres. My inspector will accompany you to your bedroom.'

'And into the bathroom too?'

'Yes, into the bathroom too, I'm sorry. I shall wait here and have a word with your wife. I regret this, Monsieur Moncin, but I have no choice in the matter.'

The architect-decorator made a vague gesture, which seemed to signify:

'As you like.'

It was only as he reached the door that he turned and asked:

'May I know why—'

'Not just now, no. Presently, in my office.'

And Maigret called from the corridor to Madame Moncin, who was still in the kitchen:

'Madame, would you mind coming here, please?'

6. Sharing Out the Tweed Suit

'Got the right one this time, have you?' young Rougin had asked cheekily, as the chief inspector and Lapointe were crossing the corridor in Quai des Orfèvres with their captive.

Maigret had simply stopped, turned his head slowly, and let his gaze rest a moment on the journalist. The other man had coughed, and the photographers themselves seemed less eager in their approach.

'Sit down, Monsieur Moncin. If it's too warm in here, you may take off your jacket.'

'Thank you. I usually keep it on.'

And indeed it was difficult to imagine him looking dishevelled. Maigret had taken off his own jacket before going through to the inspectors' office to issue instructions. Stooping slightly, his neck hunched between his shoulders, he wore an absent-minded expression.

Once in his office, he lined up his pipes, and packed two of them methodically, after signalling to Lapointe to stay and take notes of the interview. Some concert pianists take up position like this too, hesitating, adjusting the piano stool, running their fingers over the keys, as if to tame them.

'Have you been married long, Monsieur Moncin?'

'Twelve years.'

'May I ask how old you are?'

'I'm thirty-two. I was twenty when I got married.'

There was quite a long silence, during which Maigret put his hands palms down on the table.

'And you're an architect?'

Moncin corrected him:

'Architect-decorator.'

'That means, I suppose, that you're an architect who specializes in interior decoration?'

He noted that his interlocutor had coloured slightly.

'Not exactly.'

'Would you mind explaining what you mean?'

'I'm not qualified to draw up plans for a house, because I don't actually have a degree in architecture.'

'What qualifications do you have?'

'I began by doing painting, fine art.'

'When was that?'

'When I was seventeen.'

'You have your baccalaureate, do you?'

'No, when I was young I wanted to be an artist. The paintings you saw in our drawing room, they're by me.'

Maigret had not been able to work out what they represented, but they had disturbed him by their sad and morbid character. Neither the lines nor the colours were clear. The dominant shade had been a purplish-red, combined with curious shades of green that made him think of light under water, and it was as if the oil paint had spread by itself, like an ink-stain on a blotter.

'So you don't have any architectural qualifications, and if I understand you correctly, anyone can set themselves up as an interior decorator?'

'I note the generous way you describe it. I suppose you're trying to make me understand that I'm a failure.'

There was a bitter smile on his lips.

'You'd be within your rights. Other people have told me so,' he went on.

'Do you have many clients?'

'I prefer to have just a few, people who believe in me and give me carte blanche, rather than to have a lot of clients who would oblige me to make compromises.'

Maigret tapped out his pipe and lit another. Rarely had an interview got off to such an unpromising start.

'You were born in Paris?'

'Yes.'

'Which district?'

Moncin hesitated.

'The corner of Rue Caulaincourt and Rue de Maistre.'

In other words, right in the centre of the area where the five murders and the attempted attack had taken place.

'And you lived there for a long time?'

'Until my marriage.'

'Are your parents still alive?'

'Just my mother.'

'And she lives . . .?'

'Still in the same building where I was born.'

'Are you on good terms with her?'

'My mother and I have always got on well.'

'And what did your father do, Monsieur Moncin?'

Another hesitation, whereas Maigret had noticed none when his mother was mentioned.

'He was a butcher.'

'In Montmartre?'

'At the same address I just gave you.'

'And he died . . . ?'

'When I was fourteen.'

'Did your mother sell the business then?'

'She had someone handle it for a while, then she sold it, but she kept the building and lives in an apartment on the fourth floor.'

There was a discreet knock at the door. Maigret went out to the inspectors' office and returned accompanied by four men all about the same age, height and general appearance as Moncin.

They were all clerks at the Préfecture, whom Torrence had hastily assembled.

'Would you stand up, Monsieur Moncin, and go and line up with these gentlemen against the wall?'

A few minutes passed during which nobody spoke, and finally there was another knock at the door.

'Come in!' Maigret called.

Marthe Jusserand appeared, surprised to find the room so full of people. She looked first at Maigret, then at the men standing in a row, and frowned as soon as her eyes lighted on Moncin.

They all held their breath. She had turned pale, for she suddenly realized the responsibility on her shoulders. She was so conscious of it that she appeared on the point of weeping with stress.

'Take your time,' said Maigret, encouragingly.

'That's him, isn't it?' she whispered.

'You should know better than anyone else, because you're the only person who saw him.'

'I think it's him. Yes, I'm sure. And yet . . .'

'And yet?'

'Can I see him in profile?'

'Would you stand sideways, please, Monsieur Moncin?'

He obeyed without moving a muscle of his face.

'I'm almost sure. He wasn't wearing the same clothes. And his eyes didn't have the same expression.'

'This evening, Mademoiselle Jusserand, we'll take you both to the place where you saw your assailant, under the same lighting and possibly with the same clothes.'

His inspectors were combing the embankments, Place Maubert and all the usual haunts of Paris tramps, in search of the jacket with the missing button.

'You don't need me any more now?'

'No, mademoiselle. Thank you for coming. Monsieur Moncin, you may sit down again. Cigarette?'

'No thank you, I don't smoke.'

Maigret left him with Lapointe on guard, and the inspector had been told not to question him, or speak to him, and to answer vaguely if he should ask any questions himself.

In the inspectors' office, Maigret met Lognon, who had come to ask for instructions.

'Could you go into my office and just take a look at the man sitting there with Lapointe?'

Meanwhile, he made a brief call to Coméliau, and dropped in on the chief, bringing him up to date. When he caught up again with Inspector Hard-done-by, the other man was frowning, with the look of someone vainly trying to remember something.

'You know him?'

Lognon had been working in the Grandes-Carrières police station for twenty-two years, and he lived five hundred metres from the house where Moncin had been born.

'I'm sure I've seen him somewhere before. But in what surroundings?'

'His father was a butcher on Rue Caulaincourt. He's dead, but the mother still lives in the same building. Come with me.'

They took one of the Police Judiciaire's small cars and an inspector drove them to Montmartre.

'I'm still trying to think. It's infuriating. I'm sure I know him. I'd even swear we'd had contact of some kind . . .'

'Did you give him a ticket for anything, some minor offence?'

'No, it's not that. It'll come to me.'

The butcher's shop was quite a large one, with three or four assistants and a plump woman at the till.

'Shall I come up with you?'

'Yes.'

The lift was cramped. The concierge came hurrying when she saw them entering it.

'Who do you want?'

'Madame Moncin.'

'Fourth floor.'

'Yes, I know.'

The building, although clean and well-kept, was never-theless a couple of notches down from the bourgeois house on Boulevard Saint-Germain. The lift shaft was nar-rower, as were the doors, and the stairs, waxed or polished, were uncarpeted; most of the doors carried visiting cards rather than brass plates.

The woman who opened the door to them was much younger than Maigret had expected and very thin, so nerv-ous that she was actually twitching.

'What do you want?'

'Detective Chief Inspector Maigret from the Police Judi-ciaire.'

'Are you sure it's me you want to speak to?'

She was as dark as her son was fair, with small bright eyes and a few stray hairs on her upper lip.

'Come in, then, I was just tidying up.'

The apartment was nevertheless in apple-pie order. The rooms were small. The furniture must date from its own-er's marriage.

'Did you see your son last night?'

That was enough to make her stiffen.

'What do the police want with my son?'

'Could you answer my question, please?'

'Why would I have seen him?'

'I suppose he sometimes comes to visit?'

'Often.'

'With his wife?'

'I don't see that that's any of your business.'

She didn't ask them to sit down, and stayed standing her-self, as if she hoped their conversation would be brief. On the walls were photographs of Marcel Moncin at various ages, some taken in the countryside, and some drawings and naïve paintings which he must have done as a child.

'Did your son call on you yesterday evening?'

'Who says so?'

'He did come, then?'

'No.'

'Not later at night either?'

'He's not in the habit of visiting me in the middle of the night! Are you going to tell me what these questions mean, yes or no? I warn you, I won't answer. I'm in my own home, I have the right to say nothing.'

'Madame Moncin, I'm sorry to inform you that your son is suspected of having committed five murders during the last few months.'

She turned on him, ready to leap at his throat.

'*What* did you say?'

'We have reason to think that he is the man who has been attacking women in the streets of Montmartre and that he tried again, unsuccessfully, last night.'

She began to tremble, and he had the feeling, without any clear reason, that she was play-acting. It seemed to him that her reaction was not the normal one for a mother who had suspected nothing of the kind.

'And you dare to accuse my Marcel! But I can tell you it's not true, he's innocent, he's as innocent as . . .'

She looked at the childhood photographs of her son, and clenching her fists, went on:

'Just look at him! Take a good look and you won't dare say such monstrous things!'

'Your son has not been here in the last twenty-four hours, then?'

She repeated forcefully:

'No, no and no!'

'When did you last see him?'

'I don't know.'

'You don't remember his visits?'

'No.'

'Tell me, Madame Moncin, did he have any serious illnesses as a child?'

'Nothing worse than measles and bronchitis one time. What are you trying to get me to say? That he's insane? That he has always been mad?'

'When he got married, you gave your consent?'

'Yes. I was rather stupid. I even . . .'

She didn't finish the sentence, but seemed to cut herself off short.

'You arranged the marriage?'

'That doesn't matter.'

'And now you don't get on with your daughter-in-law?'

'What business is that of yours? My son's private life doesn't concern anyone, do you hear? Not you, not me. If that woman . . .'

'If that woman . . .'

'Nothing. Have you arrested Marcel?'

'He's in my office at Quai des Orfèvres.'

'In handcuffs?'

'No.'

'Are you going to take him to prison?'

'Possibly. Probably, even. The young woman he attacked last night has recognized him.'

'She's lying. I want to see him. I want to see her too, I'll soon tell her . . .'

This was the third or fourth sentence she had left unfinished. Her eyes were quite dry, though shining with fever or fury.

'Wait a moment. I'm coming with you.'

Maigret and Lognon looked at each other. She hadn't been asked to come. She was the one making decisions suddenly, and they heard her in the next room, where the door stood ajar, changing her dress and taking a hat out of a box.

'If you don't wish me to accompany you, I'll go by Métro.'

'I should warn you that the inspector will stay here and search the flat.'

She looked at the skinny Inspector Lognon as if she wanted to grab him by the scruff of the neck and push him down the stairs.

'Him?'

'Yes, madame. If you wish everything to be by the book, I'm willing to sign a search warrant for him.'

Without replying, but muttering indistinctly, she made for the door, saying to Maigret:

'Come along, then!'

And from the landing to Lognon:

'As for you, I've seen you somewhere before. And if by any chance you break anything or disarrange my cupboards . . .'

For the whole journey in the car, as she sat beside Maigret, she was muttering to herself:

'Ah no, this can't be happening, I'll go to the top, I'll see the Minister, I'll go to the President of the Republic if I have to . . . and the newspapers, I'll see that they publish what I tell them . . .'

In the corridor at the Police Judiciaire, she saw the photographers at once, and when they aimed their lenses at her, she marched straight at them with the clear intention of seizing their cameras, so that they had to beat a retreat.

'This way.'

When she found herself in Maigret's office, where the only occupants were Moncin and a drowsy-looking Lapointe, she stopped dead, stared at her son in some relief, and said, without rushing towards him, but enveloping him with her protective gaze:

'Don't be afraid, Marcel. I'm here now.'

Moncin had stood up and gave Maigret a look heavy with reproach.

'What have they been doing to you? They haven't hurt you, have they?'

'No, Mamma.'

'They're mad! I tell you, they're out of their minds! But I'll get you the best lawyer in Paris, never mind the cost. I'll give him all my money, I'll sell the house, I'll beg in the streets if I have to.'

'Mamma, do calm down.'

He hardly dared glance at her, and seemed to be apologizing to the policemen for his mother's attitude.

'Does Yvonne know you're here?'

She was peering round for her. How was it that at a time like this, her daughter-in-law wasn't at her husband's side?

'Yes, she knows, Mamma.'

'What did she say?'

'Madame, if you would sit down.'

'I don't need to sit down. What I want is to get my son back. Come along, Marcel. You'll see, they won't dare keep you here.'

'I regret to tell you that we will, madame.'

'So you're arresting him?'

'I'm holding him here to assist us with our inquiries.'

'It comes to the same thing. Have you given any thought to this? Do you realize the responsibility you are taking? I warn you, I'm not going to stand for this, I'll move heaven and earth—'

'Would you kindly sit down and answer a few questions, madame.'

'No, I won't answer anything!'

And this time, she went over to her son and kissed him on both cheeks.

'Don't worry, Marcel. Don't let them scare you. Your mother is here. I'll take care of you. You'll soon be hearing from me.'

And, glaring at Maigret, she headed determinedly for the door. Lapointe looked as if he were waiting for instructions. Maigret signed to him to let her go, and they heard her in the corridor shouting something at the reporters.

'Your mother seems very attached to you.'

'I'm all she has left in the world.'

'Was she very fond of your father?'

He opened his mouth to answer, but thought better of it, and Maigret thought he could understand.

'What kind of man was your father?'

Another hesitation.

'Was your mother not happy with him?'

To this, he spat out with deep bitterness in his voice:

'He was a butcher!'

'You were ashamed of him?'

'Inspector, I beg you not to ask me questions like this. I can see what you're getting at, and I can tell you that you're barking up the wrong tree. You can see the state you've got my mother into.'

'She got herself into a state all on her own.'

'I presume that, at Boulevard Saint-Germain or somewhere, your men are putting my wife through the same treatment?'

This time, Maigret chose not to reply.

'She has nothing to tell you. Any more than my mother. Or me. Question me as much as you like, but leave them alone.'

'Sit down.'

'Again? Will this take long?'

'Probably.'

'I suppose I've no right to have anything to eat or drink?'

'What would you like?'

'Some water.'

'You wouldn't prefer beer?'

'I don't drink, beer, wine or spirits.'

'And you don't smoke,' said Maigret thoughtfully.

He took Lapointe over to the door.

'Start questioning him gently at first, without getting to the heart of the matter. Talk to him about the suit; ask him what he was doing on the 2nd of February and the 3rd of March and all the other dates of the Montmartre murders. Find out whether he goes to see his mother on set days, and what time of day or evening, and why the two women don't get on.'

Then he went off himself to have lunch, sitting alone at a table in the Brasserie Dauphine, where he ordered a veal stew that gave off an aroma of good home cooking.

He telephoned his wife to say he wouldn't be home, and was on the point of telephoning Professor Tissot. He would have liked to see him and chat as they had at Pardon's. But Tissot was a man as busy as himself. And anyway, Maigret had no precise question to put to him.

He was melancholy and depressed for no particular reason. He felt that they were really almost there. Matters had moved faster than he had dared to hope. Marthe Jusserand's reaction had been significant. And if she had not been more categorical, it was because she had scruples. The story of giving the suit to a tramp was entirely unconvincing. And in any case, they would soon hear about it, since the central Paris tramps were not very many in number and were mostly well known to the police.

'You don't need me any more, boss?'

This was Mazet, who had played the role of presumed suspect, and now had nothing left to do.

'I called in at headquarters. They let me take a look at the man. You think he's the one?'

Maigret shrugged his shoulders. Above all, he wanted to understand. It's easy enough to understand a man who has stolen, or who has killed in order not to be captured, or out of jealousy, or in a fit of rage, or to get his hands on an inheritance. Crimes of that kind, everyday crimes after a fashion, sometimes made him feel sad, but rarely disturbed him.

'Imbeciles,' he usually grunted. Since he claimed, like some of his illustrious predecessors, that if criminals were intelligent, they wouldn't need to commit murder.

But he was nevertheless capable of putting himself in their place, reconstituting their train of thought, or their sequence of emotions.

Faced with a Marcel Moncin, however, he felt like a greenhorn, and this was so true that he had not yet dared press the questioning too far.

This was not a man like others he had encountered, men who had infringed the laws of society and more or less consciously placed themselves on its margins.

Moncin was different: he was a man who killed for none of the reasons that other people would understand, and in an almost childish way, before slashing the garments of his victim with a knife, as if it gave him pleasure.

In some sense, yes, he was intelligent. His childhood did not appear to have been particularly abnormal. He had married, and seemed to be on good terms with his wife. And if his mother was somewhat excessive, there were nevertheless affinities between them.

Did he realize it was all up with him? Had he realized it this morning, when his wife had woken him and informed him that the police were waiting for him in the drawing room?

What were the reactions of a man like this? Was he suffering? In between his crises, did he feel shame, or hate for himself and his instincts? Or, on the contrary, did he feel a certain satisfaction in supposing himself to be different from other people, a difference which perhaps in his own mind amounted to superiority?

'Coffee, Maigret?'

'Yes.'

'A cognac?'

No! If he drank spirits, he would be drowsy and he was already feeling heavy, as almost always happened at a certain point in the investigation, when he tried to identify with the people he was confronting.

'Looks like you've got him, then?'

He looked up with inquiring eyes at the owner of the restaurant.

'It's in the midday papers. They appear to think this time it's the right man. Led you a dance, didn't he! Some people were saying he was like Jack the Ripper, he'd never be caught.'

Maigret drank his coffee, lit a pipe and went out into the warm air, which seemed to stand still, imprisoned between the paving stones and the slate-coloured sky.

A man with the appearance of a down-and-out was sitting on a chair in the inspectors' office, cap in hand, and wearing a jacket entirely out of keeping with the rest of his clothes.

It was Marcel Moncin's famous jacket.

'Where did you find him?' Maigret asked his colleagues.

'By the Seine, near Pont d'Austerlitz.'

He put no questions to the tramp, only to the inspectors.

'And what does he say?'

'That he found this lying on the embankment.'

'When?'

'Six o'clock this morning.'

'Where are the trousers?'

'They were in the same place, apparently. Two of these men, they're pals, decided to split the suit between them. We haven't got the one with the trousers yet, but it won't be long.'

Maigret went over to the tramp, leaned over and noticed that there was indeed a cigarette burn on the lapel.

'Take the jacket off.'

He wasn't wearing a shirt underneath, only a ragged vest.

'Sure it was this morning, are you?'

'Yes, I am. My pal, he'll tell you, Big Paul. These gents here, they all know him.'

Maigret knew him too, and he passed the jacket to Torrence.

'Take it to Moers. I don't know if it's possible, but he might be able to work out whether the cigarette burn is recent or not. Tell him that in this case, it's a matter of the last forty-eight hours. Got it?'

'Yes, understood, boss.'

'If that lapel was burned last night or this morning . . .'

He pointed to his own office.

'Where've they got to in there?'

'Lapointe has had beer and sandwiches brought up.'

'For both of them?'

'The sandwiches, yes. The other one just drank Vichy water.'

Maigret pushed open the door. Lapointe, sitting at the desk, was leaning over the paper on which he was making notes, and thinking up his next question.

'You shouldn't have opened the window. It just brings more warm air in.'

Maigret went over to close it. Moncin followed him with his eyes, with a reproachful air, like a defenceless animal being tormented by children.

'Let me see.'

He glanced over the notes, questions and answers, which told him nothing new.

'No further developments?'

'The lawyer, Maître Rivière, telephoned to say he would handle his defence. He wanted to come over at once. I told him to contact the examining magistrate.'

'Good, that was the thing to do. Anything else?'

'Janvier phoned from Boulevard Saint-Germain. He's found in the office some scrapers of various models that could have been used for the crimes. In the bedroom he found a pocketknife with a safety catch, quite a common model, with a blade of less than eight centimetres.'

The pathologist who had carried out the autopsies, Doctor Paul, had spoken at length about the murder weapon, which had intrigued him. Normally crimes of this kind are committed with butcher's knives, carving knives, daggers or stilettos.

'From the shape and size of the wounds, I'd be inclined to say this was done with a quite ordinary pocketknife,' he'd said. 'Of course a pocketknife would have bent back on itself, so it had to be a model with a safety catch. In my view, the weapon wouldn't look very dangerous in itself. What makes it lethal is the skill with which it is used.'

'We've found your jacket, Monsieur Moncin.'

'On the embankment?'

'Yes.'

He opened his mouth, then shut it again. What had he been going to ask?

'Have you had enough to eat?'

The tray was still there, with half a ham sandwich uneaten. The bottle of Vichy water was empty.

'Tired?'

He gave a resigned half-smile in response. Everything about this man, including his clothes, was in half-tones. He had retained from his teenage years an air of timidity and amiability, difficult to describe. Maybe it had to do with his blond hair, fair skin and blue eyes, or perhaps with fragile health?

Tomorrow, no doubt, he would be in the hands of the doctors and psychiatrists. But it would be wise not to hurry things. Afterwards it would be too late.

'I'll take over,' Maigret said to Lapointe.

'Can I go?'

'Wait next door. Let me know if Moers comes up with anything.'

Once the door was shut, he took off his jacket, slumped into a chair and put his elbows on the table. For perhaps

126

five minutes, he let his gaze rest on Marcel Moncin, who had turned his head and was staring out of the window.

'Are you very unhappy?' he murmured at last, as if reluctant to speak.

Moncin gave a start, and avoided looking at him for a moment before replying:

'Why would I be unhappy?'

'When did you discover you were different from other people?'

The young man's face twitched, but he managed to give a sharp laugh:

'You think I'm not like other people?'

'When you were younger . . .'

'Well?'

'You had already realized?'

Maigret had the feeling at that moment that if he could only find the right words, the barrier would fall between him and the man across the desk, who was holding himself rigid on the chair. He hadn't imagined the twitch of the face. A shift had happened for a few seconds, and it would not have taken much for tears to come to Moncin's eyes.

'You must know that there's no risk you will go either to the scaffold or to prison.'

Had Maigret made the wrong move? Chosen the wrong words?

The man in front of him had stiffened once more, and was back in control of himself, looking absolutely calm.

'There's no risk of anything at all, because I'm innocent.'

'Innocent of what?'

127

'What you're accusing me of. I have nothing more to say to you. I shall answer no more questions.'

It was not an idle threat. Maigret could sense that he had taken a decision and would now stick to it.

'As you wish,' sighed the chief inspector, pressing the bell.

7. In the Lap of the Gods

Maigret made a grave mistake. Would anyone else in his position have been able to avoid it? That was a question he often asked himself after the event, and of course he never found a satisfactory answer.

It must have been about three thirty in the afternoon when he went up to the laboratory and Moers asked him:

'Did you get my note?'

'No.'

'I just sent it, and you probably passed the messenger on your way up. The burn on the jacket is no more than twelve hours old. Do you want me to give you details . . . ?'

'No. You're sure about that?'

'Certain. But I'll do a few tests. I presume there's no objection to my burning the jacket in a couple of other places. Some test burns would be evidence if it goes to court.'

Maigret nodded and went back downstairs. By now, Marcel Moncin would be in the Criminal Records section for the usual checks, and would have to strip for an initial medical examination and measurements, then, after dressing again, but without a tie, he would be photographed full face and in profile.

The papers were already printing the photographs taken by the reporters when he had arrived at Quai des Orfèvres, and inspectors, also now armed with his picture, were once more patrolling the Grandes-Carrières neighbourhood, endlessly asking the same questions of employees of the Métro, local shopkeepers, and anyone else who might have seen the interior decorator the day before, or at the time of the other attacks.

Maigret got into one of the cars in the courtyard and had himself driven to Boulevard Saint-Germain. The same maid as in the morning answered the door.

'Your assistant is in the drawing room,' she announced. She meant Janvier, who was alone there, putting the finishing touches to the notes taken during his search.

Both men were equally tired.

'Where's the wife?'

'About half an hour ago, she asked permission to go and lie down.'

'How did she act the rest of the time?'

'I haven't seen much of her. Now and then, she'd come and peer into the room where I was to see what I was doing.'

'You haven't questioned her?'

'You didn't tell me to.'

'I suppose you haven't found anything very interesting?'

'I chatted with the maid. She's only been here six months. The couple didn't have many visitors, and didn't go out a lot. They don't seem to have any close friends. Occasionally they spend a weekend with her parents, who have a villa in Triel and live there all year round.'

'What kind of people are the parents?'

'The father was a pharmacist on Place Clichy, and retired a few years ago.'

Janvier showed Maigret the photograph of a group in a garden. It showed Moncin, wearing a light summer jacket, and his wife in a cotton dress, alongside a man with a pepper and salt beard and a buxom woman beaming vacantly, her hand resting on the bonnet of a car.

'Here's another. The young woman with the two children is Madame Moncin's sister, who married a garage-owner in Levallois. They have a brother too, he's in Africa.'

There was a whole box full of photographs, mostly of Madame Moncin, including one of her on the day of her first communion, and the inevitable wedding photograph of the young couple.

'A few business letters, not many. He doesn't seem to have had more than about a dozen clients. Some bills. As far as I can see, they don't pay them until the tradesmen have sent two or three demands.'

Madame Moncin, who had perhaps heard Maigret arrive, or been alerted by the maid, appeared in the doorway, her features looking more drawn than in the morning, and it was clear that she had done her hair again and applied fresh make-up.

'You haven't brought him back?' she asked.

'Not until he gives us a satisfactory explanation for certain coincidences.'

'You really think it was him?'

He did not reply, and for her part she did not launch into any vehement protestations, merely shrugged her shoulders.

'One day you're going to realize that you've made a big mistake, then you'll be sorry for all the distress you've caused him.'

'Do you love him?'

Hardly was the question out of his mouth than he thought it stupid.

'He's my husband,' she replied.

Did that mean she did love him, or that, as his wife, it was her duty to stand by him?

'Have you taken him to prison?'

'No, not yet, he's at police headquarters. We'll be asking him some more questions.'

'What does he say?'

'He refuses to answer. You really have nothing to tell me, Madame Moncin?'

'No, nothing.'

'You do realize, don't you, that even if your husband is found guilty, as I have every reason to believe, he is unlikely to go to the guillotine, or to receive a prison sentence with hard labour. I told him this just now. I am quite sure the medical experts will declare that he is not responsible for his actions. A man who kills five women in the street, and then tears their clothes, is sick. When he's not in a state of crisis, he may well deceive those around him. He certainly does practise some deceit, since no one seems to have harboured any suspicion about his behaviour. Are you listening to me?'

'Yes. I'm listening.'

She might have been listening, but it was as if this conversation did not concern her, and was nothing to do with her husband. She was even following with her eyes a fly that was crawling up the net curtain.

'Five women have died so far, and as long as the killer,

or the maniac, or the insane person, call him what you will, remains at large, other lives are at risk. Do you realize this? And do you also realize that if, until now, he has attacked only unknown women who happened to be in the street, that might change, and tomorrow he might start to attack people close to him. Are you not afraid?'

'No.'

'You don't think that for months, and possibly for years, you have been in mortal danger?'

'No.'

It was discouraging. Her attitude was not even one of defiance. She remained calm, almost serene.

'You've seen my mother-in-law? What did she say?'

'She protested energetically. May I ask why you and she are not on good terms?'

'I don't wish to talk of such matters. They are not important.'

What else could he do?

'Come along, Janvier.'

'You're not going to send my husband back to me?'

'No.'

She saw them to the door and closed it behind them. That was almost all for the afternoon. Maigret went to eat with Janvier and Lapointe, while Lucas took his turn to remain alone with Marcel Moncin in Maigret's office. Then they had to resort to subterfuge to remove the suspect from the building, since a mass of journalists and photographers had colonized the corridors and anterooms.

A few large drops of rain fell on the pavements at

about eight o'clock, and everyone hoped for the thunderstorm to break, but if it did, it must have been out somewhere to the east, where the sky remained a poisonous black.

They had no need to wait for the exact time at which the previous night's attack had happened, since by nine o'clock the streets were just as dark and the lighting exactly the same.

Maigret came out alone on to the grand staircase, chatting with reporters. Lucas and Janvier pretended to be taking Moncin to the Mousetrap, in handcuffs this time, but once they were downstairs, they went into the courtyard, where they made him get into a car.

They all met up at the corner of Rue Norvins, where Marthe Jusserand was already waiting with her fiancé.

It took only a few minutes. Moncin was taken to the exact spot where the young policewoman had been attacked. They had made him wear the jacket with the cigarette burn.

'There was no more light than now?'

The policewoman glanced around and nodded.

'That's right. It was just like this.'

'Now try to look at him from the angle you saw him.'

She bent her head in various directions, and had them move the man to different positions.

'Do you recognize him.'

Appearing deeply upset, her chest heaving, she whispered, after a brief glance at her fiancé who was keeping discreetly to one side:

'It's my duty to tell the truth, isn't it?'

'Yes, it's your duty.'

Another glance seemed almost to beg Moncin's forgiveness, as he stood waiting, seemingly indifferent.

'Yes, I'm sure it was him.'

'You formally recognize him?'

She nodded her head and suddenly this young woman who had been so brave burst into tears.

'I won't be needing you again tonight. And thank you, mademoiselle,' said Maigret, shepherding her towards her fiancé. 'You heard that, Monsieur Moncin?'

'Yes, I heard.'

'You've nothing to say?'

'No, nothing.'

'Take him back, men.'

'Goodnight, boss.'

'Goodnight, everyone.'

Maigret got into one of the police cars.

'Take me home, Boulevard Richard-Lenoir.'

But this time he stopped the car at Square d'Anvers to drink a beer in a brasserie. His own role was virtually over now. In the morning, Coméliau, as examining magistrate, would no doubt wish to question Moncin, and would then send him for psychiatric tests.

At Quai des Orfèvres, it would just be a matter of following routine, contacting witnesses, asking them questions, compiling as complete a file as possible.

Why Maigret should have felt dissatisfied, though, was another matter entirely. Professionally, he had done all that was required of him. Only he had not yet understood. The 'click' had not happened. At no moment had he had the feeling of any human contact between him and the interior decorator.

The attitude of the younger Madame Moncin worried him too. He would try once more with her.

'You look exhausted,' Madame Maigret remarked. 'Is it really over?'

'Who says so?'

'The papers. And the radio.'

He shrugged. After all these years, she still believed what was printed in the papers!

'In a sense, it's over, yes.'

He went into the bedroom and began undressing.

'I hope that you'll be able to lie in a bit tomorrow morning.'

He hoped so too. He wasn't so much tired as sickened, without being able to say quite why.

'Are you upset?'

'No. Don't worry. You know it often gets me this way in this kind of case.'

The excitement of the chase no longer existed, and it was as if he was plunged into a kind of void.

'Pay no attention. Just pour me a little glass of something so that I'll sleep like a log for ten hours.'

He didn't look at the clock before going to sleep, and tossed restlessly for a while, in sheets that felt damp already, as a dog barked persistently somewhere nearby.

He had no sense of the time, or of anything else, even where he was, when the telephone rang.

He let it ring for some time, then stretched out his hand

so clumsily that he knocked over a glass of water on the bedside table.

'Hello . . .'

His voice was hoarse.

'Is that you, boss?'

'Who's that?'

'Lognon here. Forgive me for disturbing you . . .'

There was a note of sadness in Inspector Hard-done-by's voice.

'Yes. I'm listening. Where are you?'

'Rue de Maistre.'

And, dropping his voice, Lognon went on, as if regretfully:

'There's been another murder . . . A woman . . . Knifed, yes. Her dress was slashed . . .'

Madame Maigret had put the light on.

She saw her husband, who had been lying down until then, sit up and rub his eyes.

'Are you sure? Hello? Lognon?'

'Yes, I'm still here.'

'When? And anyway, what time is it now?'

'Ten past midnight.'

'When did this happen?'

'About three quarters of an hour ago. I tried to get you at headquarters. I was alone on duty.'

'I'm on my way . . .'

'Another?' his wife asked.

He nodded yes.

'But I thought the murderer was under lock and key?'

'Moncin is in the Mousetrap. Get me headquarters on the line, while I get dressed.'

'Hello? Is that the Police Judiciaire? Detective Chief Inspector Maigret wants a word . . .'

'Who's speaking?' grunted Maigret. 'Mauvoisin? You've already heard from Lognon? I presume our man hasn't budged, has he? What? . . . You've just checked? All right, I'll handle this. Can you send me a car right away? . . . To my home address. Yes.'

Madame Maigret understood that the best thing to do in the circumstances was to say nothing, and she opened the sideboard to take out the plum brandy, handing a glass to her husband. He drank it off automatically, and she followed him on to the landing, listening to his footsteps going down the stairs.

On the drive there, he did not open his mouth, looking straight ahead of him, and once he was out of the car and surrounded by a group of about twenty people, in an ill-lit section of Rue de Maistre, he slammed the car door behind him.

Lognon came to meet him, with the look of someone announcing a death in the family.

'I was at the station when they called me, I came straight over.'

An ambulance was parked at the side of the road, and its attendants were waiting for instructions, their white coats patches of light through the darkness. A few bystanders were there as well, speechless and aghast.

A female shape was lying on the pavement, almost up

against the wall, and a trickle of blood zigzagged away from it, already congealing.

'Is she dead?'

Someone approached him, a local doctor, as Maigret later ascertained.

'I counted at least six stab wounds,' he said. 'I could only examine her superficially.'

'All in the back?'

'No, at least four in the chest. And one across the throat which seems to have been made after the others and probably after the victim was already on the ground.'

'The coup de grâce,' Maigret said grimly.

Could it not be said that this murder had delivered a sort of coup de grâce to him too?

'There are shallower cuts on the forearms and hands.'

That made him frown.

'Do we know who she is?' he asked, pointing to the dead woman.

'I found her identity card in her bag. Jeanine Laurent, a domestic servant, working for a couple called Durandeau, Rue de Clignancourt.'

'How old?'

'Nineteen.'

Maigret preferred not to look at her. The little skivvy had certainly put on her best frock, sky-blue tulle, almost a ballroom dress. No doubt she'd gone out dancing. She was wearing high-heeled shoes, one of which had come off her foot.

'Who raised the alarm?'

'I did, sir.'

It was a bicycle patrol officer, patiently awaiting his turn.

'I was doing my rounds with my partner here, when I saw her lying on the left-hand pavement.'

He had witnessed nothing of the attack. When he bent over the corpse, it was still warm, and blood was still flowing from the wounds. Because of that, he had thought at first that the girl was not dead.

'Have her taken to the morgue and call Doctor Paul.'

And to Lognon:

'You've given instructions?'

'I got hold of all the men I could to comb the district.'

But what was the use? It had already been done before, without result. A car screeched to a halt, and young Rougin leaped out, his hair sticking up on end.

'Well, my dear chief inspector, what now?'

'Who tipped you off about this?'

Maigret was angry and aggressive.

'Someone from the street. There are people in this world who believe in the usefulness of the press. So, you *still* haven't got the right man?'

Without paying any more attention to the inspector, the journalist hurried over to the pavement, followed by his photographer, and while the latter took pictures, he was questioning the bystanders.

'Take care of the rest of it,' Maigret muttered to Lognon.

'You don't need anyone?'

He shook his head and got back into the car, head bowed, as if trying to digest some uncomfortable reflections.

'Where to, sir?' the driver asked.

Maigret looked at him without finding an answer.

'Just go down towards Place Clichy. Or Place Blanche.'

There was nothing for him to do at Quai des Orfèvres. What else could be done that had not already been tried?

Nor did he have the heart to go back home to a comfortable bed.

'Wait here for me.'

They had reached the bright lights of Place Clichy, where the café terraces were still illuminated.

'What can I serve you, sir?'

'Anything you have.'

'Beer? Cognac?'

'Get me a beer.'

At a neighbouring table, a platinum blonde, her breasts largely revealed by her tightly fitting dress, was trying to persuade her companion to take her across the street into a nightclub with a flashing neon sign.

'You won't regret it, I promise you. It might cost a bit, but . . .'

Did he understand what she was saying? He was either an Englishman or an American, and kept shaking his head and saying 'No! No!'

'Can't you say anything else? "No! No!" What if I said "No!" as well and just left you?'

He merely smiled placidly at her, and, losing patience, she called the waiter and ordered more drinks.

'And bring me a sandwich. Since he won't take me to supper over the way.'

Other customers were discussing the sketches of a revue

they had seen in a nearby cabaret. An Arab was hawking peanuts. An old woman selling flowers recognized Maigret and preferred to inch away.

He smoked at least three pipes without budging, watching the passers-by, the taxis in the street, hearing snatches of conversation, as if he needed to plunge back into everyday life.

A woman of about forty, overweight but still attractive, sitting alone at a small table with a crème de menthe in front of her, was smiling at him invitingly, evidently unaware of his identity.

He raised his hand for the waiter.

'Same again,' he ordered.

He had to give himself time to calm down. Just now, up in Rue de Maistre, his first instinct had been to rush back down to the Mousetrap, go into Marcel Moncin's cell and shake him until he confessed.

'Own up, you piece of filth, it was you!'

He was so certain of this that it felt like physical pain. It was impossible that he could have been wrong from start to finish. And now it was neither pity nor curiosity that he felt for the would-be architect. It was anger, almost fury.

It evaporated gradually in the cool of the night air, and from contact with the life of the street.

He had made a mistake, he knew that. And now, at last, he knew what it had been.

It was too late to make up for it, because a young woman had died, just a country girl like thousands of others who came every year to try their luck in Paris, a girl who had gone out to dance after spending all day toiling in someone else's kitchen.

It was even too late to verify the idea that had come to him. At this time of night, he would find nothing. And if any clues existed, if there was any chance of finding witnesses, it could wait till the morning.

His men were as harassed as himself. The whole case had been going on too long. When they read the paper next morning, in the Métro or on the bus, on their way in to Quai des Orfèvres, they would all experience the same stupefaction and despair that had overcome Maigret himself earlier that night. And perhaps some of them would start losing faith in him.

Lognon, when he had telephoned, had sounded embarrassed. And in Rue de Maistre he had almost seemed to be expressing his condolences.

He could just imagine Coméliau's reaction and the imperious phone call the magistrate would make as soon as he opened his newspaper.

Treading heavily, he went to the counter for a telephone token. It was to call his wife.

'Oh, it's you?' she said in surprise.

'It was just to tell you I won't be back tonight.'

For no particular reason, in fact. He had nothing to do immediately, except stew in his own juice. He felt the need to be back in the familiar surroundings of Quai des Orfèvres, in his office, with a few of his men.

He had no wish to sleep. There would be time for that when this was well and truly finished, and then he might even decide to apply for some leave.

It was always the same story. He would promise himself a holiday, then when the time came, he would find excuses to stay in Paris.

'How much, waiter?'

He paid and made his way back to the little car.

'To headquarters!'

There he found Mauvoisin and two or three others, one of them eating salami and washing it down with red wine.

'No, don't disturb yourselves on my account. No more news?'

'Same as before. They're questioning passers-by. They've arrested a couple of foreigners without proper papers.'

'Telephone Janvier and Lapointe. Ask them both to get here by five thirty in the morning.'

For about an hour, sitting alone in his office, he read and reread the transcripts of all the statements, in particular those given by Moncin's mother and his wife.

After that, he collapsed into an armchair and, unbuttoning his shirt, seemed to nod off facing the window. Perhaps he did indeed snatch some sleep. He wasn't aware of it. At any rate, he did not hear Mauvoisin come into the office at some point and then tiptoe back out.

The windows paled, the sky turned grey, then blue, and finally the sun appeared. The next time Mauvoisin came in, he brought a cup of coffee which he had brewed over a gas-ring, and Janvier had just arrived. Lapointe would soon be here.

'What's the time?'

'Five twenty-five.'

'Are they here?'

'Janvier is. Lapointe . . .'

'Just arrived, boss,' called Lapointe's voice.

Both of them had shaved, whereas the overnighters had stubble and shadow on their cheeks.

'Come on in, both of you.'

Would it be another mistake not to contact the examining magistrate? If so, he'd take responsibility for it and cover the others.

'Janvier, you're going to go to Rue Caulaincourt. Take a colleague along, doesn't matter who, whoever's the most rested.'

'To see the old lady?'

'That's right. Bring her down here. She'll make a big fuss, and probably refuse to come.'

'Certain to.'

He handed Janvier a sheet of paper which he had just signed, pressing the nib hard enough to break it.

'You just hand her this summons. As for you, Lapointe, your job is to go and fetch Madame Moncin, the wife, from Boulevard Saint-Germain.'

'Do I need a summons too?'

'Yes. Though in her case, I doubt it'll be necessary. Put the two of them together in one office, make sure to lock the door, and come back to me.'

'The Baron and Rougin are out in the corridor.'

'Oh, for God's sake.'

'Does it matter?'

'It's all right, it doesn't matter if they see them.'

The two officers went into the inspectors' room, where the lights were still on, and Maigret opened the door of his closet, where he always kept some shaving tackle. He shaved himself, slightly cutting his top lip.

'Is there any more coffee, Mauvoisin?' he called.

'In just a minute, boss. I'm making another round.'

Outside, the first tug-boats were starting up, setting out along the Seine to fetch the string of barges they would be towing up- or downstream. A few buses crossed Pont Saint-Michel, which was almost deserted. Near the bridge, an angler was sitting on the embankment, his legs dangling over the dark water.

Maigret began walking to and fro, avoiding the corridor and the reporters, while the inspectors took care not to ask him anything, or even to look him in the face.

'Lognon hasn't phoned?'

'He called around four o'clock, to say there was nothing new to report except that yes, the girl had been dancing, in a club near Place du Tertre. She went there every week, didn't seem to have any regular sweetheart.'

'And she left there alone?'

'That's what the waiters thought, though they weren't sure. They said they thought she was a good girl, not flighty.'

From the corridor came a shrill female voice, but the words were indistinguishable.

A few seconds later, Janvier came into the office, looking like a man who has just accomplished an unpleasant duty.

'Done! But what a palaver!'

'She was in bed?'

'Yes. First of all, she would only talk through the front door, and refused to open it. I had to threaten to fetch a locksmith. In the end, she put on a dressing gown.'

146

'And you waited while she dressed?'

'On the landing. She still refused to let me into the apartment.'

'Is she on her own at the moment?'

'Yes, here's the key.'

'Go and wait for Lapointe in the corridor.'

It took another ten minutes before the two inspectors returned together to Maigret.

'Both in there?'

'Yes.'

'Did any sparks fly?'

'They just exchanged one look and pretended not to know each other.'

Janvier hesitated, then risked a question:

'What should we do now?'

'For the moment, nothing. Sit in the next office, near the door between the two. If they decide to start talking, try to hear what they say.'

'And if they don't?'

Maigret made a vague gesture. It seemed to mean:

'It's in the lap of the gods now.'

8. Moncin's Show of Temper

By nine o'clock neither of the two women, locked in a tiny office, had uttered a word. Perched on upright chairs, since there was no armchair in the room, they were sitting absolutely still, as if in a doctor's or dentist's waiting room without the resource of a magazine.

'One of them got up to open the window,' Janvier told Maigret when he asked for news, 'then she sat down again, and now there's nothing more to be heard.'

Maigret had not thought about it, but one of them at any rate must be in ignorance of the previous night's murder.

'Have some newspapers taken in. Just put them on the desk as if it was routine, and arrange them so that they can see the headlines from where they're sitting.'

Coméliau had already telephoned twice, the first time from his home, where he must have read the paper over his breakfast, and the second time from the Palais de Justice.

'Tell him I've been seen in the building and that someone's gone to look for me.'

One important question had been resolved by the inspectors whom Maigret had sent out early to investigate. For Moncin's mother, the answer was simple. She could easily enter or leave her building on Rue Caulaincourt at any time of the day or night without troubling the concierge, since as a householder she had her own key. Her concierge turned out the light in the lodge and went to bed at ten, or at latest ten thirty, every night.

On Boulevard Saint-Germain, the Moncin couple, as tenants, did not have a front-door key. Their concierge went to bed later, at about eleven. Was that why, until last night, the attacks had always taken place fairly early in the evening? But when she was not in bed, and the street door was not locked, the concierge paid little attention to tenants returning from an evening at the cinema or theatre, or a night out with friends.

In the morning, she opened the street door at about half past five, to drag the dustbins out on to the pavement, then went in to get dressed. Sometimes she went back to bed for an hour.

That explained how, after the failed attack, Marcel Moncin could have left the house without being seen, to get rid of the suit by leaving it on the Seine embankment.

Would his wife have been able to go out the previous night, and return fairly late, after midnight perhaps, without the concierge remembering pulling the door-release?

The inspector who had been over to Boulevard Saint-Germain replied that yes, she could.

'The concierge says no, of course,' he explained to Maigret. 'But the other tenants don't agree. Since she's been widowed, she's got in the habit of having a couple of glasses of some sort of liqueur from the Pyrenees at night. You sometimes have to ring two or three times to get her to open the door and then she does it almost in her sleep, without hearing the tenants say their names as they go past.'

Other elements of information were arriving one after another, some by telephone. They learned, for instance, that Marcel Moncin and his wife had known each other since childhood and had gone to the same neighbourhood school. One summer, when Marcel was nine, the pharmacist's wife from Boulevard de Clichy had taken him on holiday with her children to a villa they were renting in Étretat in Normandy.

It was also discovered that after their marriage, the young couple had lived for a few months in an apartment which Madame Moncin senior had made available to them in the building she owned on Rue Caulaincourt, on the same landing as herself.

At half past nine, Maigret took a decision:

'Go and fetch Moncin from the Mousetrap. Unless he's already in Coméliau's office.'

Janvier, from his listening post, had heard one of the two women get up, and then the rustle of pages of a newspaper. He did not know which of the women it was. But still no sound of voices.

The weather was bright once more, the sun was shining, but it felt less sultry than the previous days, as a light breeze was rustling the leaves on the trees and sometimes lifting a paper on the desk.

Moncin entered the room without a word, looked at Maigret, whom he greeted with a very slight inclination of his head, and waited to be invited to sit down. He had been unable to shave, and his light-coloured stubble blurred the sharp outlines of his face. He looked less clear-cut, his features were vaguer, from exhaustion as well, no doubt.

'You have been informed of what happened last night?'

He replied as if reproachfully:

'Nobody has spoken to me at all.'

'Read this.'

Maigret passed him the newspaper which had printed the most detailed account of the attack in Rue de Maistre. While the prisoner was reading, the inspector did not take his eyes off him, and he was sure he was not mistaken: *Moncin's first reaction was indignation.* He had frowned, looking surprised and irritated.

Despite the arrest of the interior decorator,
another victim has been killed in Montmartre.

He appeared to think for a moment that this was a trick, perhaps a fake newspaper, concocted on purpose to get him to confess. He read it carefully, checked the date at the top of the page, and finally accepted that this report was true.

Did he not seem to be bursting with a kind of repressed anger, as if something had been spoiled?

At the same time, he was obviously trying to understand, and appeared finally to find the solution to the problem.

'As you see,' Maigret said, 'someone is trying to save you. And too bad if that has cost the life of some poor girl who'd just arrived in Paris.'

Did a furtive smile cross Moncin's lips? He struggled to suppress it, but it was visible all the same, a childish glee, quickly stifled.

'Both women are here,' said Maigret laconically, affecting not to look at Moncin.

This was a strange struggle, such as he could not remember ever having had in the past. Neither of them was on firm ground. The least nuance would count, an expression, the trembling of a lip, the blink of an eyelid.

If Moncin was tired, this was even more the case for Maigret, and furthermore, he was full of disgust. He had been tempted once again simply to send the case straight to the examining magistrate and let him sort it out.

'They will be brought in shortly, and you will have to explain things to each other.'

What was Moncin's reaction at that moment? Fury? Possibly. His blue eyes glared more fixedly, he clenched his jaw, and directed at Maigret a reproachful glance. But perhaps there was fear in that expression too, since at the same time beads of sweat broke out, as they had the previous day, on his forehead and upper lip.

'Are you still determined to say nothing?'

'I've nothing to say.'

'Don't you think it's time all this came to an end? Don't you think, Moncin, that there has been at least *one crime* too many? If you had spoken up yesterday, this one wouldn't have happened.'

'It has nothing to do with me.'

'*You* know, don't you, which of those two women stupidly decided to save you?'

He wasn't smiling now. On the contrary, he looked more angry, as if he were resentful of the woman who had acted.

'I'm going to tell you what I think of you. You're sick, in all probability, since I cannot believe that a man with a normal mind would act as you have. The psychiatrists will have to settle that question. Too bad for you if they declare that you are responsible for your actions.'

He was still watching the other man's reactions.

'Admit it, you would be seriously offended if they declared that you are *not* responsible for your actions?'

And indeed a gleam of anger seemed to have crossed Moncin's pale eyes.

'Never mind. So, you were a child like any other, at least that was how things appeared. The son of a butcher. Did you feel humiliated to be the son of a butcher?'

No need for an answer.

'It humiliated your mother too, and she saw in you a sort of aristocrat, somehow living in Rue Caulaincourt. I don't know what your father looked like, the ordinary hardworking butcher. All those photographs that your mother has piously kept, yet I didn't see a single one of him. She's ashamed of him, I suppose. You, on the other hand, from a tiny boy, you were photographed at every stage, and when you were six years old, an expensive costume was specially made for you, to go as a marquis to a fancy dress party. Do you love your mother, Monsieur Moncin?'

Still no answer.

'Did it eventually become oppressive to you, being

pampered like this, made much of, treated like a delicate creature needing constant care?

'You could have rebelled, cut the cord, as so many others in that situation would have. Listen to what I'm saying. Other people will be handling you from now on, and they won't treat you with kid gloves.

'To me, you are still a human being. Don't you see that that is precisely what I want to get you to show: just a tiny spark of human feeling?

'But you didn't rebel, because you are lazy, and because you have a sense of overweening pride.

'Other people may be born into titles, money, servants and a life of luxury.

'You were born to a mother who had to be all that to you.

'If ever anything happened to you, your mother would be there for you. You knew that. You could do anything you pleased.

'Only there was a price to pay: you had to be docile.

'You belonged to your mother. You were her plaything. You didn't have the right to grow up into a man like other men.

'Was it your mother, afraid you might start gadding about, who arranged to get you married off at twenty?'

Moncin was staring intently at him, but it was impossible to guess at his thoughts. One thing was clear: he was flattered that someone was taking all this notice of him, that a man of Maigret's importance was considering his words, deeds and innermost thoughts.

If the inspector were to make a mistake about something, would he react, protest?

'I don't think you were in love, because you're too self-centred for that. You married Yvonne for a bit of peace and quiet, and perhaps in the hope of escaping from your mother.

'As a little girl, Yvonne was bowled over by the blond, elegant boy that you were. You seemed to be made of very different stuff from your schoolmates, for all that you were the son of a butcher.

'And your mother was deceived by that. She saw Yvonne just as a little goose whom she could shape any way she wanted, and she installed the pair of you on the same landing as herself in the building she owned, so as to keep you under her wing.

'But none of this explains why someone would go out and kill people, does it?

'The real explanation won't come from the doctors, who will only be able, like me, to shed light on one aspect of the problem.

'You are the only one who knows the whole story.

'But I don't think you will be able to put it in words.'

This time he was rewarded by a slightly defiant smile. Did that mean that, if he wanted to, Moncin could perfectly well make his acts understandable to other people?

'I'm coming to the end. The little goose turned out not only to be a real woman, but as possessive a female as your mother. Between the two of them, it became a tug-of-war, with you as the prize, and there's no doubt you were being pulled one way and the other.

'Your wife won the first round, because she managed to get you out of Rue Caulaincourt and transplant you to the apartment on Boulevard Saint-Germain.

'She gave you a new horizon, new surroundings, new friends, and from time to time you escaped to go back to Montmartre.

'Did you start then to develop towards Yvonne the same resentment you'd felt for your mother?

'*The pair of them were preventing you from being a real man, Moncin!*'

The prisoner threw him a glance full of rancour, then looked down again at the floor.

'That's what you imagined, that's what you tried hard to believe. But at heart, you knew quite well it wasn't true.

'You simply didn't have the courage to be a man. You weren't one. You needed those women, you needed the atmosphere they had created around you, with their fussing, their admiration and their indulgence.

'And that was precisely what humiliated you.'

Maigret went over to the window to take a breath, and mopped his forehead with his handkerchief, his nerves as on edge as those of an actor impersonating a desperate character.

'You won't reply. Very well, I know why it is impossible for you to reply: it would be too painful for your self-respect. Owning up to your cowardice, to the continual compromises you have had to make, would be too agonizing.

'How often did you feel like killing them? I don't mean the poor girls you killed in the street, I mean your mother and your wife?

'I'd be prepared to bet that when you were a boy, or a youth, the idea sometimes entered your head of killing your mother, so as to be free.

'Not a real plan of action, no. Just one of those thoughts that cross our minds and are then forgotten, that we put down to a moment of rage.

'And then the same thing happened all over again with Yvonne.

'You were their prisoner, a prisoner of both women: they fed and cared for you, they cosseted you, but at the same time they possessed you. You were their plaything, their treasure, and they fought each other over you.

'Between Rue Caulaincourt and Boulevard Saint-Germain, you became a shadow of a man, so as to have a bit of peace.

'When did it happen, what was the emotional shock, what sudden humiliation stronger than before was the trigger? I don't know. You're the only person who could answer that, and I'm not even sure that you can.

'But you formed a plan, vague at first, then becoming clearer and clearer in your mind, to assert yourself in some way.

'How could you assert yourself?

'Not in your profession, because you are well aware that you've always been a failure in that respect, or worse, an amateur. Nobody takes you seriously.

'How, then? By some dramatic act?

'Because to satisfy your pride it had to be something spectacular. Something everyone would talk about, that would give you the sensation of soaring high above the crowd.

'Was it at that point that you got the idea of killing the two of them?

'Only that was too dangerous a game. Any investigation

157

would inevitably focus on you, and there would be no one left to support you, flatter you and encourage you.

'And yet it was these two, the dominant females, that you hated.

'And it was females, picked at random, that you attacked in the street.

'Did it bring you some kind of relief, Moncin, to find you were capable of killing? Did it give you a sense that you were superior to other men, or simply that now you were a man?'

He looked Moncin sternly in the eye, and the other man almost tipped his chair over backwards.

'Because murder has always been considered the greatest of crimes, and some people might think it requires exceptional courage.

'I suppose the first one, on the 2nd of February, brought you a moment of relief, a kind of intoxication.

'You'd taken precautions, because you didn't want to pay the price, you didn't want to go to the scaffold, or to prison, or to some mental institution.

'Monsieur Moncin, you are a *bourgeois criminal*, a sissy, a criminal who needs his comforts and little luxuries.

'That is why, ever since I set eyes on you, I've been tempted to use the methods the police get blamed for a lot. Because you're afraid of blows, afraid of physical pain.

'If I were to hit you with the back of my hand, you'd collapse, and who knows whether you wouldn't prefer to confess than get another blow?'

Maigret must have looked terrifying, unintentionally, because of the anger that had been mounting gradually inside him: Moncin, shrinking in his seat, had turned ashen-faced.

'No need to be afraid, I'm not going to hit you. In fact, I'm not sure that it's really you that I am most angry with.

'You proved you were intelligent. You picked an area of Paris that you knew like the back of your hand, as only those who grew up there could have.

'You chose a silent weapon, and at the same time it was one that gave you physical satisfaction at the moment of impact. It wouldn't have felt the same pulling the trigger of a gun or pouring poison into a glass.

'You needed a furious, violent act. You wanted to destroy and feel that you were destroying.

'You stabbed, but that wasn't enough: you went into a frenzy of rage afterwards, like a child.

'You slashed the victim's dress and her underclothes, and no doubt the psychiatrists would see that as symbolic.

'You didn't rape your victims, because you're incapable of that, because you've never really been a man.'

Moncin suddenly raised his head, and stared at Maigret, gritting his teeth as if he was about to leap at him.

'Those women's dresses, their petticoats, bras and panties – all that represented femininity and you wanted to tear it to pieces.

'What I'm asking myself now is whether one of the two women suspected you, not necessarily the first time, but after that.

'When you went to Montmartre, did you tell your wife you were going to see your mother?

'Didn't your wife perhaps establish a connection between the murders and these visits?

'You see, Monsieur Moncin, I will remember you all my life, because in my entire career no case has disturbed me so much, or taken so much out of me.

'After your arrest yesterday, neither of them assumed you were innocent.

'And one of them decided she was going to save your life.

'If it was your mother, she had only a short distance to go to get to Rue de Maistre.

'If it was your wife, that means she was prepared, supposing we let you go, to live side by side with a killer.

'I haven't rejected either of those hypotheses. The two women have been here since early this morning, sitting opposite each other in an office, and neither one of them has opened her mouth.

'The one who committed the murder knows she did it.

'The one who is innocent knows that the other is not, and I wonder whether she isn't secretly feeling jealous.

'Hasn't there been a struggle, a tug-of-war between them, going on for years, to see which one will love you most, possess you most fully?

'And what better way to possess you than to save your life?'

The telephone rang, just as the other man was opening his mouth.

'Hello. Yes . . . Speaking . . . Yes, indeed Monsieur Coméliau . . . He's here. My apologies, but I need him for another hour. No, the press wasn't wrong . . . An hour. They are both here at headquarters . . .'

Impatiently, he hung up and went to open the door to the inspectors' office.

'Show in the two women.'

He needed to bring this to a close. If the momentum that had carried him this far did not enable him to make an end of it, he sensed that he would never get to the bottom of the case.

He had asked only for an hour, not because he was sure of himself, but as a concession. In an hour, he would pass the case over, and Coméliau could do what he liked with it.

'Come in, ladies.'

His emotion was detectable only from a certain quiver in his voice, and the exaggerated calm of some of his movements, such as holding out a chair for each of the women.

'I will not try to deceive you. Close the door, Janvier. No, don't go away, stay here and take notes. I said I won't try to deceive you and make you believe Moncin here has confessed. I could have questioned you separately. As you see, I have decided not to resort to any tricks of the trade.'

The mother, who had refused to sit down, came towards him, mouth open, and he snapped at her sharply:

'Be quiet. Not now.'

Yvonne Moncin had sat down primly on the edge of her chair, like a young lady on a social call. She had glanced briefly at her husband and now she was staring at Maigret as if she wanted not only to listen to him but to read his lips.

'Whether he confesses or not, he has killed five times, and you are both perfectly aware of that, since you know his weaknesses better than anyone else. Sooner or later, it will be established. Sooner or later, he will end up in prison or in some institution.

'One of you imagined that by committing another murder, while he was in here, she would be able to clear him of any suspicion.

'We simply need to find out now which of the two of you committed the murder last night of a certain Jeanine Laurent, at the corner of Rue de Maistre.'

At last the mother got a word in:

'You have no right to question us without a lawyer present. I forbid them both to say anything. It is our right to have legal assistance.'

'Would you please sit down, madame, unless you have a confession to make.'

'That's the limit, as if I had anything to confess! You're behaving like . . . like the uneducated lout you are, and you . . . you . . .'

During the hours she had been sitting in a tête-à-tête with her daughter-in-law, she had been silently accumulating such a volume of bile that she was losing the faculty of speech.

'I must ask you again, please sit down. If you continue to act like this, I shall have you removed elsewhere by an inspector, who will question you, while I concern myself with your son and daughter-in-law.'

That prospect calmed her down suddenly. The change was palpable. She remained for a moment open-mouthed with stupor, then looked as if she were thinking: Just you dare!

Was she not his mother? Were her rights not longer established and worth more than those of a girl whom her son had happened to marry?

He had emerged not from Yvonne's womb, but from hers!

'Not only did one of you hope to save Moncin,' Maigret now continued, 'by committing a copycat murder while he was locked up here, but I am also sure that whichever of you it was had long been aware of what he had done. So she must have had the courage to be alone, day after day, with him in a room, without any protection or chance of escape if he took it into his head to kill her too.

'And that woman loved him enough, in her way, to . . .'

The look Madame Moncin senior gave her daughter-in-law did not escape him. Never had he seen so much hatred in human eyes.

Yvonne had not moved a muscle; both hands clasped on her red leather handbag, she still seemed as if hypnotized by Maigret, not missing the slightest of his changes of expression.

'I have simply this to tell you. I can say that Moncin's head will almost certainly not roll. The psychiatrists will, as usual, disagree about his state of mind, they will argue about it in front of a jury, who won't understand a word of what they say, and there is every chance he will get the benefit of the doubt, in which case he will be sent to a mental institution for the rest of his life.'

The man's lips trembled. What was he thinking at that precise moment? He must feel terribly frightened of the guillotine, and he would also fear prison. But perhaps he was imagining the scenes inside mental institutions – or lunatic asylums, as the popular imagination paints them?

Maigret was convinced that if they could promise him a room of his own, a personal nurse, the right to special care, and the attention of some famous professor, he would willingly talk.

'But for the woman involved, it won't be the same. Paris has been living in the shadow of fear for six months, and people who have lived in such fear are not forgiving. And the jury will be made up of Parisians – fathers and husbands of women who might have been stabbed by Moncin at some street corner.

'There won't be any question of madness in her case.

'In my view, the woman will pay the full price.

'She knows this.

'One of you is that woman.

'One of you, intending to save a man, or rather, not to lose something she considered her property, was prepared to risk her head.'

'I am quite prepared to die for my son,' Madame Moncin senior declared suddenly, enunciating each syllable clearly. 'He's my child. What does it matter, what he's done? What do *they* matter, those good-for-nothing women strutting around at night in the streets of Montmartre?'

'Did you kill Jeanine Laurent?'

'I don't know her name.'

'So you committed the murder last night in Rue de Maistre?'

She hesitated, looked at Moncin, and finally said:

'Yes.'

'In that case, can you tell me the colour of the dress she was wearing?'

This was a detail Maigret had asked the press not to publish.

'I . . . it, it was too dark to . . .'

'Excuse me. You cannot be unaware that she was attacked less than five metres from a streetlamp.'

'I didn't notice.'

'But when you slashed the material of the dress . . .'

The crime had in fact been committed over fifty metres from the nearest streetlamp.

Then, in the silence, they heard Yvonne Moncin's voice, answering calmly, like a schoolgirl in class:

'The dress was blue.'

She was smiling, still sitting demurely on her chair, and turning towards her mother-in-law, at whom she now looked defiantly.

She was the one, in her own mind, who had won this battle.

'Yes, it was blue,' said Maigret with a sigh, letting his nerves relax at last.

And the relief was so sudden, so violent, that tears came to his eyes, perhaps tears of exhaustion.

'Carry on from here, Janvier,' he murmured, getting to his feet and picking up a pipe at random from his desk.

The mother had shrunk into herself, suddenly ageing ten years, as if her sole reason for existing had been snatched away.

Maigret did not look at Marcel Moncin, whose head had slumped on to his chest.

The chief inspector pushed through the crowd of reporters and photographers who mobbed him in the corridor.

'Who was it? Do we know?'

He nodded and muttered:

'By and by . . . in a few minutes . . .'

And he hurried towards the glass door leading to the Palais de Justice.

He spent barely fifteen minutes with Coméliau. When he returned, it was to issue instructions.

'Release the mother, of course. Coméliau wants to see the other two as soon as possible.'

'Together?'

'Yes, at first. He'll be the one to give a statement to the press.'

There was someone he would have liked to see, but not in his office, and not in the corridors or wards of an asylum: Professor Tissot, with whom he would have had a long conversation, like the one that evening at Doctor Pardon's.

He could not ask Pardon to organize another dinner party. And he was too tired to go over to Sainte-Anne to wait for the professor to be free to see him.

He pushed open the door of the inspectors' office, where all eyes turned to him.

'It's over, boys.'

He hesitated, looked round at his colleagues, gave them a weary smile, and admitted:

'And now I'm going home to bed.'

It was true. This did not often happen, even when he had been up all night.

'Tell the chief . . .'

Then, in the corridor, faced with the journalists:

'Go and see Coméliau. He will give you a full statement.'

They saw him plod down the stairs, alone, his back bent, and he stopped at the first landing to spend a moment or two lighting the pipe he had just packed.

One of the drivers asked him if he wanted a car and he shook his head. He wanted first of all to go and sit at the terrace of the Brasserie Dauphine, as he had long sat, that other night, at the terrace of another bar.

'A beer, inspector?'

Looking up, he replied in an ironic tone, and the irony was all for himself:

'No, two!'

He slept until six in the evening, in sheets damp with sweat, the window open on to the sounds of Paris, and when at last he reappeared in the dining room, his eyes still puffy, it was to announce to his wife:

'Tonight, we're going to the cinema . . .'

Arm in arm, as was their habit.

Madame Maigret asked no questions. She had a feeling he was coming back from a distant place, that he needed to get used to everyday life again, to rub shoulders with ordinary, reassuring people.

Other Titles in the Series

THE MISTY HARBOUR
GEORGES SIMENON

'A madman? In Maigret's office, he is searched. His suit is new, his underwear is new, his shoes are new. All identifying labels have been removed. No identification papers. No wallet. Five crisp thousand-franc bills have been slipped into one of his pockets.'

A distressed man is found wandering the streets of Paris, with no memory of who he is or how he got there. The answers lead Maigret to a small harbour town, whose quiet citizens conceal a poisonous malice.

Translated by Linda Coverdale

OTHER TITLES IN THE SERIES